The Neighbors

You Live Too Close, You Know Too Much

Disclaimer: *This is a work of fiction. All the names, characters, businesses, places, events and incidents in this book are either the product of the author's imagination or used in a fictitious manner. Any resemblance to actual persons, living or dead, or actual events is purely coincidental.*

Acknowledgements: *Without the help of the following people, this book would not be possible. I would like to thank Alyson Montione and Chelsea Carr for helping me to edit this book. I would also like to thank Deb Palmer for reading through and giving me some excellent feedback. The Schoharie Library Writing Club for helping me with ideas, details, laughter, and most importantly their unwavering support. Thank you to my family for supporting me and being my biggest fans.*

Prologue

Peter took a deep breath, knelt on one knee, and pulled out a ring. "Jessica Erin Winslett, will you be my wife?"

Jess looked at him with tears in her eyes. She was speechless and then found her voice. "Yes!" she cried happily. She wrapped her arms around him as he lifted her and spun her around in a circle.

Jess couldn't believe this was happening. Especially today of all days. She looked at the simple diamond ring on her left hand. It all seemed surreal. She looked up at Peter again.

"Why today?"

Peter took the graduation cap off her head and smoothed down her hair. He kissed her gently. "Why not today? We've just graduated from NYU. The world is our oyster. Our lives are finally about to begin. It seems to me that today is the perfect day to ask you to be my wife."

Jess wasn't so convinced. "You're going off to Harvard after the summer to pursue your law degree and I'm still going to be here working. Doesn't it seem strange to you that we'll be engaged and hundreds of miles apart?" she complained. "Don't you at least want to see if we'll survive as a couple?"

He lifted her hand and gazed at the diamond on her finger. "I don't have to wait and see. I know in my heart, it's you Jess. It's always been you. It always will be you."

She looked up at him. His dark wavy hair and brown eyes melted her heart. He wasn't just the man she loved but he was also her best friend.

Peter put his hand against her face. "It's only for three years. Harvard isn't across the country. It's just a little over two hundred miles away. We can visit. Spend weekends together. Facetime. It'll be over before you know it."

Chapter 1

That was six years ago. Now she was Jess Stanton, data analyst and wife of a very busy defense lawyer. She rolled over and turned off the alarm before it went off. Jess wasn't surprised to see Peter already out of bed. He had always been an early riser. She climbed out of bed and stretched. Then, started the shower and picked out her clothes while waiting for the water to heat up. The apartment they lived in was small and old, but she didn't mind. To her it was home, even though Peter wanted to move somewhere bigger.

Jess marveled at the thought that today was their first wedding anniversary. The smell of pancakes drew her to the kitchen. Peter was standing at the stove flipping a pancake. She stepped closer and smiled widely.

"Blueberry pancakes, my favorite. You spoil me," she said.

Peter slipped the pancake on a plate and handed it to her. "That's my plan. I wish I could stay and have breakfast with you, but I'm running late for work." He kissed her on the cheek as he picked up his briefcase and left.

That afternoon, a bouquet of red roses was unexpectedly delivered to her office. She looked at the card.

Our lives are just beginning.
Love Always,
Peter

She smiled and smelled the flowers. He definitely knew how to spoil her. When quitting time arrived, Jess eagerly collected her things and looked forward to arriving home. They could finally celebrate their first anniversary properly.

When she arrived home, Peter was waiting at the door with a glass of Pinot Noir. He was dressed in a dark pinstriped suit and his dark hair was cut short and gelled back. He leaned in and kissed her seductively.

"You know, we really don't need to go out to dinner." Jess murmured in his ear. She wrapped her arms around him and kissed him again. "I would be content with continuing this right here."

His deep chuckle warmed her heart, but he regretfully pulled away. "We can continue this after dinner. We'll consider it dessert."

Jess groaned in frustration as she walked towards her bedroom and started getting dressed for their night out. She stepped out dressed in a short black dress with dainty heels. The dress showed off her long sleek legs. Her curly dark hair was pulled up away from her face. A simple gold necklace that held a single teardrop diamond was the same one she had worn at their wedding. She smiled when she saw the wanton look on Peter's face.

"You are so beautiful," he murmured as he took her into his arms again and kissed her.

"Are you going to tell me where we're going?" Jess asked.

Peter laughed. "Now, that would ruin the surprise." He looked at his watch. "We'd better get going, though, or we're going to lose our reservation."

She was surprised when they pulled up in front of La'Pont Delagio, an expensive and very posh restaurant that took months to get a reservation.

Her eyes grew wide. "Honey, you really shouldn't have done this. This is just the first anniversary of many. Are you sure we can afford this?"

Peter didn't answer, but instead handed his keys to the valet, walked over to her side of the car, and opened her door. He placed his hand on the small of her back and led her into the restaurant. A beautiful woman in her twenties greeted them and asked for their name.

"Stanton," Peter replied. The woman turned and led them to a table for two.

The ambiance is so elegant, thought Jess, as she silently looked around the room. Peter held out her chair as she sat down at the table adorned with a white tablecloth, a flickering candle, and a vase with a single red rose and a sprig of baby's breath behind it. The sensuous sound from the violinist enveloped her, and she felt like she had stepped into an entirely different world.

After they were settled and had placed their order, Jess smiled at Peter and took a sip of her wine. She felt nervous and out of her element. Peter reached over and held Jess's hand.

"Jess? Where do you see us in five years?"

Jess thought for a minute and said, "Still married. Still happy. You'll still be a successful lawyer, maybe even a partner. I'll keep working for Ellis Incorporated. Maybe we'd even start talking about having children."

Peter looked at her earnestly. "What if I told you I see something different in five years?"

"What do you see?" she asked.

Peter lifted her hand and kissed it. "In five years, I see us with a little boy or a little girl around 4 years old. I see us living in the country with a big yard for our kids to play in. I see a house filled with laughter and a lot of love. I see myself working normal hours and spending evenings and weekends with my family."

Jess lifted her hand. "Hold up, I'm confused. I thought you liked your job. What's changed?"

Peter ran a hand through his short hair. "It's not that I don't like my job, but I feel like I need a change. Don't get me wrong, I still like being a lawyer, but I hate all the long hours. I hate coming home to you and finding you already asleep in our bed. I rarely get to hear about your day, and to be honest, I don't really think I want to become partner."

Jess shook her head, trying to clear it. "Peter, what are you saying? You becoming partner has always been our plan."

He leaned forward and said excitedly, "I have the opportunity to open up my own law office. I'd be my own boss and make my own hours for the most part."

Jess smiled broadly. "Oh honey, that's great news. I fully support you if it's what you really want to do."

Jess saw Peter's shoulders relax and was surprised that he would doubt that she would be anything but supportive of him.

"Where is the office located? Can we go see it after dinner?"

They were interrupted with the arrival of their food. It looked amazing and Jess was starving.

They each ate in silence until Jess asked again, "Where did you say the office was located?"

Peter wiped his mouth with the cloth napkin and put it aside. He reached into his suit jacket and pulled out a white envelope. He placed it in front of Jess.

"Open it," he told her excitedly.

She looked at him and smiled as she slid open the envelope. "Peter, this really is entirely over the top. I don't think there's anything else you could possibly do to-"

She stared at the picture of a Dutch colonial house with tall sleek windows setting off the gray cedar shake exterior. It was surrounded by a large yard with maple trees scattered throughout.

"It's a picture of a house?" She looked at him quizzically.

"It's our house," he said excitedly. "I bought us a house. Happy anniversary."

Jess was speechless. She stared at her husband, her fury rising by the second. "Peter, of all the asinine things you have ever done, this one takes the cake." She was practically yelling. "You bought us a house. Without discussing it with me first?"

Jess put the picture down on the table. "You honestly thought this was a good idea? Buying a house is a big deal. We've never even discussed buying a house."

People were starting to look at them. The waiter came over to the table looking concerned.

"Is everything alright?"

"No," Jess barked.

"Yes," Peter replied. "My apologies, my wife got a little carried away."

The waiter nodded and walked away.

Jess took a deep breath and said in a much quieter voice, "You spring not only this on me, but also a job change? My God, Peter, who do you think you are? Are you in this marriage alone? Because you sure are making decisions like you are."

Peter sat back, looking deflated. "That was the surprise part. I want you to have the best. After I asked you to marry me, we spent nights talking about the house we'd have and the kids we'd raise."

He stopped talking.

Jess started to calm down; she could see how much this meant to him. She reached out and placed her hand over his. "We did talk about all those things, but I thought we'd be doing them together. I thought we'd be picking out a house together. I know you meant well, Peter, you really did, but to be honest, this caught me off guard. I mean, *a house?*"

He pulled his hand out and laced his fingers through hers. "I'm sorry I jumped the gun on this. I honestly thought you'd be thrilled. I love you, Jess, and if you don't want the house, I'll put it back on the market and we'll start over together."

Jess was quietly looking at the picture of the house again. Who bought a house without consulting with their spouse? Peter, that's who. He'd always been impulsive. Just like when he asked her to marry him on their graduation day.

When he got an idea in his head, he jumped in with both feet.

Begrudgingly she asked, "Where is this house located? What about the practice you were talking about? How can we possibly do both?"

Peter smiled. "That's the best part. It's upstate and it's perfect for us." He put up his hand before she could interrupt. "Before you say anything, I got a great deal on the house. It was listed way below market value. Can you at least look at it first before you make any decisions?"

Jess felt the knots in her stomach clench even more. She knew she was on the edge of a panic attack, but this wasn't the time or the place. She knew what Peter wanted her to say, and so she said it. "A house. I can't believe you bought me a house."

She smiled at him, and even though she was still annoyed, she also knew he wanted to make her happy, and this was his way of showing it.

Chapter 2

Jess sighed with exhaustion as she pulled into the driveway of their new house. She had been driving for hours, and she had begun to think that they'd never get here. Jess always envisioned her future differently. She thought they would sell their little apartment and move near the beach. They would spend the evenings walking along the beach. Maybe they'd even have a dog that walked with them. That had always been her dream. She didn't care where she lived as long as it was near the ocean. She loved surfing and scuba diving, but most of all, she loved the sound of the waves. It always soothed her. Vacations weren't long enough. She wanted something more permanent.

Peter, on the other hand, insisted they'd love the country. He had grown up in Upstate New York and never stopped talking about it. He would bring her up skiing in the winter and leaf peeping in the fall. It was beautiful and she didn't mind spending a weekend, but she had never wanted to live there. There was no beach, no hustle and bustle, and most towns had a population of less than five thousand. Who could live like that? Not to mention the wildlife. She had heard stories of bears, coyotes, porcupines, and a barrage of other animals. Why would anyone willingly want to live amongst them? It seemed crazy to her. When she had driven closer to the house, she had to slam on her brakes to keep from hitting a deer darting out across the road in front of her car. Her heart was still racing from that one.

She had lived in a city all her life, first in Wilmington, North Carolina, and then for the last nine years in New York City. She was used to the noise and the lights. She loved meeting up with friends in the morning for coffee before work and laughing with Peter in the evening over Chinese takeout. The city was electrifying and full of life. She loved being a part of that life.

She looked out her car window at a rabbit hopping across the neatly mowed lawn. The country was alright for something different occasionally, but it meant something entirely different when she had agreed to move here. She looked up at the house that Peter had bought. It was as beautiful as the pictures. The house was offset with sleek black shutters. It had a white wrap-around porch going from the back of the house to the side of the house, overlooking the expansive yard sporting huge maple trees. The peonies and dahlias were already blooming in the flowerbeds that framed the front of the house. The yard itself was plain. There were some trees but not much else. She didn't know the first thing about gardening, but it needed sprucing up.

Although the house was beautiful, she still couldn't believe that she had agreed to move here. Peter had looked so excited when he showed her his new office on Main Street. The town was small, with little local shops displaying their wares, and lampposts with hanging flower baskets lining both sides of the street.

Once they left his office, he drove another ten minutes and proudly showed her the house. When she had walked inside, the first thing she noticed was the newly polished wooden floors. The entranceway led to a large living room with floor-to ceiling windows overlooking the back lawn. The kitchen was cozy with a rustic feel to it. Upstairs were three large bedrooms. Peter explained that they would sleep in the master bedroom, and the other two rooms would be their offices. It was a far cry from the home that she had pictured. Her vision was a simple house on the beach, where she could fall asleep listening to the waves lapping against the sand. Little white curtains waving in the warm breeze through small open windows. She was never going to have that.

As they walked through each room every part of her wanted to scream *NO, I DON'T WANT TO MOVE HERE*, but she couldn't do that to Peter. This was too important to him. Hell, he had even signed the papers for the new law office. It would have been near impossible to back out now.

She thought about the closing on their house. It was odd that the owners weren't present. She would have liked to ask them why they had listed the house so low. There had to be something wrong with it. Otherwise, why the low price?

A rabbit hopped across the yard, distracting her thoughts. She looked behind her at all the boxes piled high in the back of her car. She sighed loudly, impatiently waiting for her husband to pull up behind her. She huffed again for the thousandth time, irritated with him for only having one set of keys for the house— and of course they were in his pocket.

She glanced out her back window. Where was he? It wasn't like there was a ton of traffic driving through town. In reality, there were only a few traffic lights. Even if he hit every light, he still should have been there by now.

She stepped out of the car to stretch her legs. Maybe later, she could go for a run. Jess turned and surveyed the deserted road in front of the house, already missing the running trails in Central Park. This place didn't even have sidewalks. She looked up at the house again. She knew being the wife of a defense lawyer meant she might lose a lot of arguments, but not having a say in their life decisions was not going to be a part of this marriage. She had shared her feelings with him after their elaborate dinner on their anniversary. It had been a long night, but in the end, they had both agreed to no more secrets or surprises when it came to major life decisions. They would make those together.

She walked over and sat down on the grass under a shade tree, trying to cool off. Upstate New York in the summer heat could be just as brutal as living down south. The only difference was at least you had the ocean down south. Here the heat was just stifling, and even being in the shade didn't offer much relief. She closed her eyes and felt herself start to drift off. It had been an extremely busy month of packing and cleaning. Not only was it busy but it was also emotionally draining saying goodbye to her parents and friends. Although she had only moved three hours away, it felt like halfway around the country. These last few weeks had done her in.

Peter's truck rumbling down their gravel road brought her back to the present. She yawned and stood up, dusting herself off. The real work was about to begin. The thought of unloading and unpacking all the boxes and furniture that were shoved into the U-Haul truck made her groan. Once this was over, she didn't want to move for a very long time.

She walked over to him, trying not to look irritated at the lateness of his arrival.

Peter smiled as he opened his door and presented her with a bouquet of colorful flowers. Lilies, her favorite. He knew everything about her, including the fact that flowers always cheered her up.

"I'm sorry I'm late," he said apologetically. "I couldn't resist stopping and picking these up for you. I know what a sacrifice this is for you, and I'm grateful that you're putting your faith in me. I promise I won't let you down."

Jess's eyes filled with tears. He did know how she felt, and she knew without a doubt that he wouldn't let her down. They would get through this together, somehow.

"Thank you," she said, smelling the lilies. "They're beautiful."

She turned around and opened the hatch on the back of her car to begin unloading. Peter, on the other hand, had a different idea. He took the flowers from her and placed them on the hood of the car, then scooped her up in his arms.

She let out a squeal of laughter. "What are you doing?"

"Carrying you over the threshold, my lady."

Her heart melted, and she knew that with him by her side, everything would work out.

Chapter 3

It had taken them hours to unload all the boxes and furniture. Jess regretted not calling the moving company and insisting that they could move everything themselves. She put her hands on her hips and looked around, feeling overwhelmed at the amount of stuff they had accumulated in the years they had lived together.

Her body ached as she bent over and lifted another heavy box onto the counter. Her head was pounding, and her back wasn't going to take much more. How they had accumulated so much stuff when they lived in such a small apartment baffled her.

A doorbell chimed throughout the house, causing Jess to jump. She didn't even know the house had a doorbell, and wondered what other surprises awaited her. She dusted off her clothes and hastily ran a hand through her hair as she walked to the door. Jess peeked out the side window to see who was there, since they didn't know anyone yet. It didn't appear the person was leaving or delivering anything.

She was hesitant as she pulled open the door and came face to face with a tall, very tanned man in his mid-thirties standing in a pair of khaki shorts and a white golf shirt. He had sunglasses perched on top of his head and piercing blue eyes. He reminded her of a slick salesman.

He smiled widely at her, his white teeth gleaming.

"Hello? Can I help you?" Jess asked uncertainly.

The man held out his hand. "Hi, my name's Daniel. I'm your neighbor from next door." He motioned to his left, and she could make out the two-story blue and white house behind their tree line.

She smiled and shook his hand. "I'm Jess. It's nice to meet you."

They stood looking at one another for a moment until Jess, feeling awkward, said, "Where are my manners? Come on in, my husband is here somewhere."

Daniel stepped inside and stood against the wall. Jess tried to see the house from his perspective. She took in all of the boxes stacked precariously on the living room floor and through to the kitchen. It reminded her of a Jenga game.

He groaned, "Unpacking is always the worst, isn't it?"

Peter walked into the kitchen looking confused. "I thought I heard voices in here. I'm Peter, and you are?"

Daniel smiled and walked towards him. They shook hands. "I'm Daniel. I'm your neighbor. I just wanted to pop over and introduce myself." He scanned the boxes strewn throughout the house. "It looks like you'll be busy for some time."

Jess cleared her throat. "Would you like something to drink? We have some water or a few beers in the fridge."

"A beer would be great."

Jess grabbed three bottles out of the fridge, and all three of them walked out onto the porch. It was a warm, sunny day. The kind of day that should be spent outdoors instead of unpacking. Jess breathed in the fresh air and sat down on a wooden rocker that was left behind by the previous owners. The two men sat down opposite in matching Adirondack chairs.

"It's going to be nice having neighbors again," Daniel said. "It's been too quiet with just the wife and I."

Jess smiled and said, "We're looking forward to getting to know you and your wife, as well. This house is very different than our small apartment in the city."

They talked for a while about city life versus living in the country. Daniel told tales of some of the wildlife he's seen.

When there was a lull in their conversation, Jess said, "Say, I wonder if you could help me with something?"

"I'll try," Daniel replied.

"This is a beautiful house and the acreage that it sits on is superb. The price we paid for it was way below the asking price. Is there something wrong with it that we should know about? Is it haunted, falling apart, or something crazy like that?"

Daniel laughed. "No, not that I know of. I would say you got yourself a great deal."

Jess leaned forward in her chair looking curiously at Daniel. "Do you mind me asking what happened to them? Did die?"

Daniel looked at her curiously. "Die? Not that I know of. What makes you ask?"

"They weren't present at the signing, and the realtor couldn't give us an answer as to why. It just seems very odd."

Daniel shrugged, "Odd is a good word to describe the previous owners. They were an odd couple. They kept to themselves and weren't very friendly. We'd try to invite them over and they would always decline. We'd wave as they drove past, but they wouldn't acknowledge us. I'm sorry to say I have no idea why they moved, but I'm not going to miss them. Like I said, they weren't very friendly."

Peter said, "Well, hopefully you and your wife will have a different opinion of us. By the way, I met your wife yesterday. I stopped to buy Jess some flowers. We started talking and she asked where I bought a house. When I told her, she laughed and said we were neighbors."

Daniel nodded. "Yes, she owns The Blooming Boutique in town. She's very gifted when it comes to plants and flowers. She has been very successful. She started from a small flower stand, and now she owns her own shop. The Blooming Boutique is where everyone in town goes for their flower needs, whether it's a small occasion or a wedding." He chuckled. "Listen to me. I sound like a commercial." Daniel picked up his beer and took a swig. "I'm glad you met her. Say, in a few weeks I'm having a small gathering at our house with some close friends. You two should stop over. It'll be a great opportunity to meet the locals in town."

Jess groaned inwardly at the thought of having to go to a meet and greet with a bunch of strangers on top of all the unpacking that was left to do. She wasn't against going, but the timing just wasn't right. She didn't even know Daniel very well. She opened her mouth to speak, but Peter beat her to the punch.

"We'd love to," Peter said, draping an arm over Jess's shoulders.

"Great," Daniel replied, standing up and handing his empty bottle back to Jess. "I'll give you the details as soon as my wife tells me the details."

They all laughed as Daniel stepped off the porch and started walking towards his house.

"He seems really nice," Peter remarked.

Jess nodded. "Yes, I suppose he does."

"Is something wrong?"

Jess shrugged. "I just wish we could have discussed the party before accepting."

Peter looked at her with surprise. "Since when do you not like going out and meeting people?"

"It's not that I don't like going out and meeting people, but there's so much to do. We have all this unpacking and trying to get settled in. I'm exhausted, and now I'm going to have to smile and pretend like I'm having a good time. We don't even know these people."

Peter walked over to her and took her hands. "This is how we could get to know them," he said patiently. "This is our home now. These are our neighbors. Now is as good a time as any to become part of the community. If I want to make connections and make the business grow, then I need to network. People need to get to know us. Honey, this is just all part of the process."

Jess looked up groaning inwardly, "I know."

He pulled her in for a kiss, then said, "Plus, he said in a few weeks. It's not like you're going to a party tomorrow. We'll be settled by then. I don't see what the big deal is."

Jess bit her tongue. Peter was right. This was their home now, whether she liked it or not. She had agreed to move here with him.

They continued to unpack in silence for the next few hours. She organized kitchen drawers and put away clothes. She tried to decide where she wanted the furniture. It felt like a never-ending task, and she was dog tired. No matter what she did, the house still didn't feel like hers, and honestly, she didn't know if it ever would. It still felt like Peter's house. He had picked it out. This was where he wanted to live. Where he wanted to start a family.

Even though it had only been a day, she missed the city, and the coziness of their apartment. This felt so permanent. Her shoulders ached. Her head was still pounding, and she was tired of trying to figure out where to put things. It felt as though they were starting all over, and in a way, they were.

She closed her eyes and tried to push her resentment away. It was done. Peter had just taken a job as the town's newest attorney. In actuality, Peter was the town's only attorney, but he was excited to work for himself, and Jess was happy for him. Truly, she was, but in the back of her mind there was a nagging feeling that something wasn't right. Moving here and conveniently having a beautiful house way below asking price and a law office readily available in the same town just didn't sit right with her. It was too perfect.

She looked over at Peter unpacking. Maybe this really was what he wanted. She was his wife and she wanted to support him however she could. Maybe she should look at this as an adventure. Maybe this would be a good thing for them as a couple.

Her phone buzzed, and she reached over to see who was calling. It was her boss from Ellis Incorporated. She smiled wryly; not everything in her life had changed. Jess was able to keep her job as a data analyst and work from home. She loved her job, and she would have probably fought harder to stay in the city if she had to give it up.

"Hi, Lenore," Jess said.

"Hi, Jess. I'm sorry to bother you on a Sunday, but I was calling to see if your Internet was up and working. You have a meeting tomorrow at ten."

Jess smiled. "I'm all set, Lenore. No worries."

"Good, glad to hear it. Have a nice evening."

Jess hung up the phone and slipped it back into her pocket.

Tomorrow was Monday, and she was looking forward to getting back into the routine. She was ready to take a break from the move and get back to work.

Chapter 4

Jess stood and stretched. She'd been sitting in front of her computer for hours, going over facts and figures for work. She was supposed to meet with her client next week to go over the quarterly earnings. She looked at the clock: four o'clock. It was time for a break.

The walk to the kitchen helped to stretch the kinks out of her legs. Now, if only she could get the kinks out of her back. After some stretches Jess felt re-energized and poured herself a glass of lemonade and walked out onto the porch. The porch was one of her favorite parts of the house. She sat down on a wooden rocker and watched two squirrels chase each other up one of the maple trees. As she closed her eyes she listened to the sound of birds twittering and chipmunks chattering. It wasn't something that she was used to hearing, but lately, it made her feel at peace.

The sound of a vehicle caught her attention. She looked over in Daniel's direction and noticed a white box truck pulling into his driveway. She had noticed that, for the past week, trucks had been constantly pulling in and out. If she didn't know any better, she'd think his house was a loading station. It was bizarre.

She could hear muffled voices as two men dressed in what looked like gray uniforms got out of the truck and opened the back door. Maybe he owned some kind of company. Jess was too far away to see what the truck was hauling, but her curiosity was starting to get the better of her. She wondered what Daniel did for a living. She'd have to ask the next time she saw him.

The sound of Daniel's laughter echoed across the lawn, and Jess could see him pat one of the men on the back of the shoulder. Another man retrieved a black duffel bag and handed it to Daniel. The driver climbed back into the truck, but instead of driving away, he backed the vehicle into a mid-sized wooden barn. She guessed Daniel was using it as a garage. It seemed odd that the truck would pull into a barn instead of staying parked outside. The doors to the barn closed once the vehicle was inside, and all three men walked into the house.

Jess looked down at her watch: four thirty. Between the move and sitting in front of a computer all day, her body ached. If she hurried, she'd have time for a run before Peter got home. She walked into the house and changed into her running shorts and pink tank top. With her unruly dark hair pulled up into a ponytail and her phone strapped to her arm for music she quickly walked outside and began stretching her muscles. She was starting to feel better already.

As she jogged past Daniel's house, she could see the two men opening the barn doors and climbing back into their truck. As she jogged along to the beat of the music, the truck caught up to her. It slowed down as the men drove past her. The passenger, a man with a scar down his cheek, made eye contact with her as they passed by. The lustful look he gave her sent chills down her spine. It was unsettling. Her mind drifted back to the people who sold their house at such a low price. Maybe it wasn't them who were unfriendly, but the company Daniel kept. Something didn't feel right.

Jess turned the music up louder and turned left, continuing her run, and tried to put the occupants of the truck out of her mind. Too many crime shows on television were making her imagination run wild. *That's what happens when you're secluded and have no one to talk to* she thought. She checked her watch and saw that she had run three miles. Two more miles, and she would be back home. A five-mile run wasn't bad after staying cooped up in the house all day.

By the time Jess's house came into view, she was sweating profusely. She was happy to see that she was finishing her run in a decent time despite the heat. The sound of tires alerted Jess that another vehicle was coming up behind her and she veered off the road and into the grass.

It slowed down and passed by. It was Daniel. He put his arm out of the window in a wave as he continued past.

Jess walked across the yard, her breath slowing. It was almost time for Peter to come home. She showered, then walked into the kitchen just as he came in through the door.

"How was your day?" Peter asked as he put down his briefcase and walked over to kiss her.

"Good. How was the first day in your new office?"

He grimaced. "Slow. Apparently there's not much that happens in a small town. I drove towards Albany today to meet with lawyers there. They said they could refer me to a few cases to get me started."

"That's great news, honey. You knew you'd have to build up a reputation, and this is your ticket to doing just that. It'll get better, you'll see."

"Do you think I'm stupid?" Peter snapped. "Of course, I knew it would be slow. You have no idea what I'm going through."

Jess felt as though she'd been slapped. "Whoa, where did that come from? This was *your* idea. *You* wanted to move here. *You* wanted your own business."

She started to leave the room but whirled around and stomped back towards him. "And for your information, you have no idea what I'm going through. I'm miserable walking through this mausoleum of a house in the middle of nowhere. I have no friends, no family, no one. So don't for one minute patronize me."

"Bitch doesn't look good on you. Quit whining, you sound pathetic."

Peter walked to the refrigerator and pulled out a beer. After he popped the top, he looked at her. "Tell me when dinner is ready. I'll be in my office."

Jess picked up a plate that was lying close by on the counter, tempted to throw it at the back of his head, but she refrained. Sometimes, it was really hard to be married to a lawyer. He always wanted the last word. *He can make his own damn dinner*, she thought.

She needed to get out of there. Maybe go for a drive? Where would she go? There was nowhere to go. Jess did the only thing she knew to do. She calmly walked upstairs and changed into another set of running clothes. A run would help extricate the frustration and anger she was feeling. She started off at a jog, but soon began quickening her pace. She felt stuck. Stuck in her marriage. Stuck in this place. Stuck in her life. How did she end up here?

She thought about Peter. He wasn't like this. When they were dating, he was always so thoughtful. He never called her names, and they hardly ever fought. When her brother died of an overdose, Peter was her rock. This was new.

When Jess got home, she was appalled at the mess that Peter left in his wake. The counter was littered with empty beer bottles. He must of run out, because there was also a half bottle of Jim Beam sitting out. She started cleaning up, hating herself for doing it. But she had always cleaned up Peter's messes, and this was no different.

Jess thought back to when she would invite her friends over. Peter would always instigate an argument, which abruptly resulted in her friends leaving. She would try to smooth things over, but in the end, it was easier to just not invite her friends over anymore. In the city, Peter liked to live richer than his finances allowed. Jess tried to talk to him about it, but eventually she took on an extra job to pay the bills. When she tried to talk to him about it, he would tell her that he was doing everything for her. They were a team and shared their finances, so it wasn't unreasonable to have her chip in to pay the bills.

This too shall pass, Jess thought to herself. Once Peter started getting clients and his law business was running more smoothly things would go back to how it once was. She was sure of it.

****

The next day, Jess was on a conference call listening to a new advertising client explain what they wanted analyzed. The sound of a truck rattling down the dirt road distracted her. She looked up at the clock. It was still early. Jess glanced out the window. Through the trees she noticed another box truck, this time black, pull up to Daniel's barn and drive inside. Once again, two men got out of the truck, handed Daniel a duffel bag, and closed the barn door behind them.

"Jess? Are you still there?" the client asked.

Jess shifted her attention back to the computer. "My apologies. I thought I heard something, but it must have been the wind. Please, go on."

Once the meeting was finished, she walked outside and sat down in one of the rocking chairs on the porch, watching as the truck drove away. *Daniel sure has a lot of deliveries at his house,* she thought to herself.

Something back by the tree line caught her attention. It wasn't moving and it was definitely not part of the yard.

Jess stood up and slowly walked towards the unidentified object, praying that whatever it was wouldn't attack her. She bent down and picked up a branch that had fallen on the ground for protection if she needed it. *Better safe than sorry.* She stepped closer, not realizing that she was holding her breath until she let it out in relief. The little lump lying on the ground was a golden retriever puppy, curled up in a ball and fast asleep.

Jess looked around, trying to see who the puppy belonged to, but saw no one. The branch dropped to the ground as she bent down to pet its soft fur. The puppy began to stir and opened his sleepy eyes. He stretched and yawned, sticking out his pink tongue.

"Where did you come from?" Jess asked as she picked him up. The puppy began to wriggle and wag its tail. She laughed and sat down on the grass. He climbed onto her lap and plopped down, completely content.

"You have to belong to someone. Let's see if we can find your owner."

Jess picked up the pup and walked over to Daniel's house. It had to be his pup-- he was her only neighbor.

She rang the doorbell and waited.

Daniel answered the door. "Jess, what a nice surprise. Is there something I can help you with?"

Jess held out the pup. "I believe this little guy belongs to you. He wandered into my yard."

Daniel looked puzzled as he studied the pup at a distance. "No offense, but I'm not a dog person. It isn't my dog."

"It isn't my dog either. Where could it have come from? It's just a puppy."

Daniel shrugged and said, "Somebody must have dumped him here. People do that sometimes. Their dog has a litter, and they can't take care of all the puppies or choose not to care at all, and dump off the litter on the side of the road. This little fella--" he lifted the pup from Jess to look at him closer-- "Must have wandered into your yard."

"What am I supposed to do with him?" asked Jess, bewildered.

Daniel handed him back to Jess. "Whatever you want. You can drop him off further down the road, keep him, take him to a shelter, you pick."

Jess groaned. "Thanks, I'll talk to Peter and figure out what we should do with him."

She started walking away, then turned around just before Daniel closed the door. "Daniel?"

"Yes."

"I never asked, what is it that you do for a living? You look too young to be retired."

His eyes met Jess's. "I'm in sales."

"Really? Do you work from home?"

He was still smiling, but his eyes turned to a hard gray steel. Jess got the sense he didn't like this line of questioning. She tried to sound nonchalant.

"I only ask because I'm a data analyst and work directly with sales departments." She motioned towards her house. "I work from home most days."

He looked at her and motioned towards the pup. "Well, good luck with whatever you decide to do with the canine. It's been nice chatting, but there's some work I need to finish up."

"Oh, sorry. I didn't mean to keep you."

Well, that was awkward, thought Jess, as she walked back towards the house.

Peter turned into the driveway and shut off his truck. He smiled when he spotted Jess walking from Daniel's house, then frowned when he saw the puppy in her hands.

He walked toward her. "Hi, honey. I see you have a puppy. Where did you get that?"

Jess smiled and nuzzled the pup's head. "He was just sitting in our yard."

Peter rolled his eyes. "Just sitting, was he? We live miles from town and not a person in sight besides Daniel, and there's a pup just sitting in our yard saying 'Come claim me'?"

Jess blew out a breath of exasperation at the sarcasm in his voice. "I walked outside, and this puppy was alone and sleeping at the edge of the tree line. I took it to Daniel's house to see if it belonged to him. It didn't. Daniel said it's not uncommon for people to drop animals off on the side of the road and drive off. That must have been what happened. Can you believe someone would do that?"

The puppy whined. Jess looked down. "Oh, you poor thing. You must be hungry. Let's go inside and get you something to eat and drink."

Jess was filling the pup's water dish when Peter walked through the kitchen. He spied the food and water dishes, shook his head, and muttered, "Just what we need."

Chapter 5

Victoria turned in the mirror to look at the nasty bruise forming on the back of her left shoulder. Once again, Daniel had lost his temper and took it out on her.

She had been late coming home from The Blooming Boutique the day before, and dinner wasn't ready. He was sitting in the living room staring at the door when she came in. Victoria had taken one look at Daniel and known he was in a bad mood. She forced a smile and walked over to kiss his cheek.

"Hi, honey. Dinner will be ready soon."

She walked into the kitchen to start the salmon. She wasn't going to have time to prepare something fancy. She had thought just salmon, lemon-roasted baby potatoes and a salad would be sufficient. She was wrong. He had taken the plate and thrown it in the trash. Then he grabbed her by the hair.

"Where have you been?" he'd demanded.

"Working," she replied. "It's the end of the month and I had to balance the books."

He pulled her hair harder and pushed her up against a wall.

"I don't believe you," he spat.

She didn't cry or show fear. He hated weakness, and especially when she cried. She had learned that the hard way.

He had let go of her and stomped off towards the living room. She breathed a sigh of relief when he released her.

Apparently, something must have gone wrong with the drop, or more likely, the money that was owed to him must have been short. That always brought out the worst in him.

She didn't dare ask about his day; instead, she went upstairs to change out of her work clothes. She tried to stay out of his way, but he wasn't through with her yet. He had followed her upstairs.

Victoria stretched out her arm and grimaced as a sharp pain on her shoulder blade shot through her. Maybe she'd make him a special dinner. He'd like that.

As she looked in the closet for something to wear for work, she spotted the royal blue sleeveless dress that she'd planned to wear at their party. It was hanging on a hook behind the door. She moved it to the back of the closet, knowing she wasn't going to be able to wear it by Saturday. With a heavy sigh, she took down a green half sleeve dress instead. It wasn't as festive, actually it was quite plain in comparison-- but she didn't have much choice.

After Victoria was dressed, she studied her face in the mirror. As always, Daniel had left her face alone. He was always so careful about leaving bruises in places where they wouldn't be seen. She didn't look bad for a woman in her mid-thirties. Her red wavy hair still held its natural color. Her 5'7 stature was taller than many of the women she knew, and her long, flowing skirt gave her the impression of being willowy. She slid on her stylish sunglasses, which masked her eyes. The red marks around her neck were almost nonexistent. Once again, Daniel knew just when to let go.

Her boots clicked through the empty rooms as she grabbed her purse, pulled out the keys, and left the house without another look back.

Victoria knew that Daniel was watching her out the window as she climbed into her car. He always watched her after they had a fight, but that was last night, and it was in the past. She'd forgive him. She always did. He needed a strong woman in his life, and Victoria made sure she was everything he could have wanted in a woman. Sure, he'd lost his temper, but she knew what to do. She knew how to act. She knew what was expected of her.

As she drove away, she knew that when she came home Daniel would have a beautiful piece of jewelry as a peace offering. Daniel was always so sweet after they had a fight.

When Victoria entered The Blooming Boutique, her heart swelled with pride. It was the one thing that was all hers. The smell of flowers and plants breathed new life into her, and the vibrant colors brightened her mood considerably. She opened the door and started moving some of her plants outside. A cute planter placed in the center of an empty table. Another planter on a chair, then she placed flower displays strategically around the doorway. Once the open sign was placed in the window, she walked through the back room towards her office. Her office was the one place she hated. It was small and dimly lit, located in the back of the store, and closed off from everything. It made her feel claustrophobic.

Victoria walked towards the closet where the safe was stored and punched in her combination. The door swung open, displaying piles of cash that Daniel had deposited in there. It was her job to launder his money through her business. She didn't like to do it, but if it let her keep The Blooming Boutique and Daniel didn't meddle in any of her business dealings, then it was a small concession to pay. She took out money for her cash register, then closed the doors and locked them again. Once she was out of her office, she turned and locked that door as well. She looked at the clock. It was nine o'clock. She unlocked the store door and turned her sign to *Open*.

The morning passed quickly as she began making more planter displays, and then walked over to the cooler and pulled out some roses, baby's breath, and greenery for wedding bouquets that would be picked up in a few days.

The bell chimed above the door as Mrs. Avery shuffled inside. She was a shorter woman, with short gray hair and round glasses. She always reminded Victoria of Mrs. Claus. Victoria smiled and waved at her.

"Good afternoon, Mrs. Avery. It's nice to see you again."

"Thank you dear. I see you have new asters this week."

Mrs. Avery came into The Blooming Boutique every Wednesday afternoon after her bridge game. As usual, she brought with her one of her famous homemade blueberry muffins and handed it to Victoria.

"I know it's your favorite," she said, smiling.

"Thank you, Mrs. Avery. You know my weakness," Victoria replied, taking the muffin from the older woman and peeling back the wrapping.

Victoria continued, "In addition to the asters, I also have many colorful dahlias, and in that back corner are my new flower arrangements." She motioned towards the back of the store. "Have a look around, you might find something to add to that beautiful garden of yours."

Mrs. Avery began wandering through the store, every once in a while picking up a plant for further inspection. She seldom bought anything, but always liked to know the latest gossip. She picked up another plant. "How's that handsome husband of yours doing?"

Victoria forced a smile. "He's fine, as usual."

Mrs. Avery smiled. "And how's business been?"

Victoria swallowed a bite, then said, "Fine, as usual."

Victoria knew Mrs. Avery's questions by heart, but she also knew the old widow didn't have much to do during her day, so she was always patient with her.

Mrs. Avery picked up a small pot with ivy leaves cascading over the side. She pretended to study it as she asked nonchalantly, "I heard your new neighbors moved in next door. What are they like?"

Victoria laughed and said, "Now Mrs. Avery, they just moved in a few weeks ago. Let them get settled in before they become the talk of the town."

Mrs. Avery set down the plant and walked over to the counter where Victoria was polishing off the last of her muffin. "So, you haven't met them yet? Victoria, where are your manners? I would have been there with a plate of muffins welcoming them to the neighborhood."

Victoria put up a hand. "I've been busy, Mrs. Avery, but don't worry, we'll have them over in a couple of weeks once they get settled in."

Mrs. Avery was beaming as she gossiped, "I heard the husband, his name is Peter Stanton, took over Leroy Sutton's law office. I guess we've got a new lawyer in town."

Victoria nodded. "I met Peter when he drove through town. He stopped to buy his wife some flowers. He seemed very nice. I think they'll be a nice addition to our little town."

"He bought his wife flowers? How romantic. It will be nice to have new people in town." Mrs. Avery looked down at her watch. "Well, I should get going. I'm meeting Betty at the diner for coffee."

Victoria waved as Mrs. Avery left. She knew that the Stantons were going to be the topic of conversation at the diner. By dinner, the news of Peter's romantic gesture of buying his wife flowers would be all over town.

She thought back to the night she met Peter Stanton. He seemed nice enough. She had noted a touch of arrogance, but that was just her first impression. She hoped she was wrong, and they could all be friends. She didn't have many of those, although she had many acquaintances through her business. Most of the people she would consider a friend were wives of Daniel's friends. It made it convenient to do things together like go out on the boat, motorcycle rides through the mountains, or day trips wine tasting, but she didn't have anyone she could open up to or depend on. She wondered if she ever would.

On the outside, Daniel treated her like a queen, and he made sure everyone knew it. For the most part, she *felt* like a queen, unless he was in a bad mood, which didn't happen frequently, thank goodness. She'd learned lessons the hard way, but now she knew what Daniel expected, and she did her best to not disappoint him.

Chapter 6

Saturday morning, Jess woke up and got dressed for her run. Sampson, the pup, stood next to the door waiting. He was too little to run with her, but she couldn't resist those big brown eyes.

Peter walked in and poured himself a cup of coffee. "I thought you were going for a run."

Jess turned and smiled. "I changed my mind. I want Sampson to start learning how to stay with me. He can eventually be my running partner. So instead, we're going for a walk."

Jess opened one of the kitchen drawers to take out the leash. The drawer was sticking. She pulled harder and wiggled the drawer back and forth. Looking inside, she saw a piece of paper wedged between the drawer and the runners. She reached in and grabbed the paper. It was ripped. There was writing scrawled across it: *If anything happens to me*...the rest of the note was missing.

Jess walked across the room and picked up a flashlight. She tried to pull out the rest of the paper, but it kept ripping into smaller and smaller pieces.

"Peter, look at this," Jess said, showing him the paper.

He looked at it and laughed.

"What's so funny?"

"It reminds me of when I was a kid. I would make my brother mad and then write a note that said if anything happens to me, it was my brother's fault."

Jess looked at him incredulously. "So, you think this is from a kid?"

"Of course, don't you?"

She looked back down at the note. "I don't know."

Jess walked into the foyer and placed the note in a desk drawer.

****

Peter sat down at the table and opened the newspaper. Jess walked over and filled Sampson's bowl with food and gave him some fresh water. When the dog was finished eating, she picked him up and nuzzled him.

"You're such a good boy." Jess picked up Sampson's leash and clicked it on to his collar.

"You act like you love that stupid dog more than me," Peter muttered.

"You're being ridiculous," Jess said. "You see people all the time. I see no one except people on a computer screen. I have no one to talk to except you. At least with Sampson around, I'm not as lonely.

"Now you're the one being ridiculous. No one is stopping you from getting out and meeting people."

Jess glared at him, then leaned down and petted Sampson. "Come on, Sampson, let's go for a walk."

She opened the door and walked outside with Sampson at her heels. Jess walked past Daniel's house and waved at Daniel who was watering his plants. He turned off the hose and walked towards Jess and the pup.

"I see you decided to keep him, huh?" he said.

Jess smiled. "Yes, I didn't have the heart to do anything else."

"What's his name?"

"Sampson."

"That's an awfully big name for such a little dog," remarked Daniel.

"He'll grow into it," Jess said, looking fondly at the pup.

"Will you and Peter be over this afternoon?"

"Of course, we're looking forward to it." She looked down the road, then back at Daniel. "Well, we'd best get going. I'll see you this afternoon."

Jess and Sampson walked side by side down the road. Once the pup began to get tired, Jess picked him up and carried him the rest of the way home.

****

Peter and Jess walked over to Daniel's house with a plate of cookies in hand.

She was looking forward to getting to know other people. She felt so isolated living here, but the closer they got to Daniel's house, the more ill at ease Jess was beginning to feel. This looked nothing like the small gathering she was expecting. There must be at least 50 people here. She felt embarrassed in her simple floral wrap-around dress, holding a plate of cookies.

Peter was dressed in casual dress pants and a light blue button-down shirt rolled up at the sleeves. He would easily fit in with this crowd. She wished she could go home and change, but it was too late for that. As a last-ditch effort, she turned to tell Peter she'd forgotten something and had to go back home, but Peter was already waving to someone.

He leaned down and whispered to Jess, "I'll be right back. I have some networking to do."

Before Jess could utter a word, she spotted Daniel walking towards her with a tall, beautiful red-haired woman.

"Jess, this is my wife, Victoria."

Jess smiled. "Hi Victoria, it's nice to finally meet you."

Victoria grinned in return. "I've been waiting months to see who our new neighbors would be. It's going to be so nice having people next to us again."

Daniel waved to a couple of men and said, "Excuse me, ladies. I'll catch up with you later."

Jess stood awkwardly with Victoria. She held out the plate of cookies.

"I baked some cookies. I apologize that there's only a small amount. When Daniel said a 'few friends' I assumed it was a small gathering."

Victoria laughed. "Daniel likes to show off, and he does everything in a big way. You'll soon learn what I mean."

They passed a buffet table filled with cakes, pies, shrimp, stuffed mushrooms and other items that were guaranteed to tantalize the tastebuds. In the middle of the table was a beautiful flower arrangement bursting with the colors of summer.

Jess motioned towards the table. "I love the flower arrangement you have on the table. I'm assuming it came from your store?"

Victoria beamed with pride. "Yes, just a little something I put together for the occasion. I met your husband when he was driving into town. I hope you're settling in alright."

"Yes, we're all unpacked. It's one of the perks of working from home."

Victoria took the cookies from Jess and placed them on the table. She filled a glass with Cabernet and handed it to Jess.

"I'll introduce you to the girls," Victoria said. "You'll love them."

Jess smiled and took a sip of wine. She hoped she didn't look nervous. Since she had been working from home, she had become a bit of a recluse.

"I'd love that. Between working from home and unpacking, I haven't had a chance to meet anyone."

Victoria led her to a small group of women sitting under the gazebo, who were laughing hysterically.

"Jess, these are the girls. She pointed from left to right. This is Amelia, Deirdre, and Evelyn. Ladies, this is Jess. She's our newest resident, who also happens to be my neighbor."

A middle-aged woman with dark hair piled on her head smiled at Jess. "Welcome, Jess. I'm Amelia. I've lived here all my life, so if you have any questions about anything, don't hesitate to ask." She took a sip of champagne, then continued, "Where are you from?"

Jess immediately began to feel at ease. "I'm originally from Wilmington, North Carolina, which is on the coast, but I've lived in New York City for the last nine years. My husband, Peter, is a lawyer, and his office was located there."

"Oh," Evelyn exclaimed. She appeared to be in her mid-twenties, with long, sleek blonde hair. "Your husband must be our newest lawyer in town. I heard he was moving up here from the city."

"That's right," Jess confirmed.

Evelyn continued, "Jess, you have a big adjustment to make. We are definitely not as glamorous as the city, and you'll be driving for quite a while before you will find a beach."

All the women laughed.

Victoria chimed in. "Well, I hope she'll adjust with no problem. I want a neighbor who I can do things with."

Jess thought back to the note she had found that morning. She looked back at Amelia. "Speaking of neighbors, can you tell me anything about the people who previously owned our house? It's a mystery. No one seems to know anything about them."

"What do you want to know?" Amelia asked.

"Did they have any children?" asked Jess.

"Children?" Amelia looked at Victoria. "Did they have any children?"

"No children," Victoria answered. She studied Jess. "Why are you so curious about the previous owners?"

Jess shrugged. "I found some things that belong to them, but I don't know how to get ahold of them. We bought the house 'as is' for what I think is a lower than typical asking price. There's got to be more wrong with the house. No one sells for the price they sold us that house. They weren't present at the signing, and the realtor didn't know of anything out of sorts with the house. It's all just a little odd."

All the women grew quiet and looked awkwardly at each other. Amelia nervously took a long sip of her champagne, and a couple of the other women excused themselves and left. Jess felt like this was a taboo subject, but no one was willing to say anything.

Before things became more awkward, Jess said, "I'm sorry, did I say something wrong? It's just that they weren't present at the closing and there was no explanation of why, which seems odd to me."

Victoria cleared her throat and spoke up. "The previous neighbors were an odd couple, Jess. Nothing like you and Peter at all. It doesn't surprise me that they didn't show up for the closing. We tried inviting them over, and they always declined. They kept to themselves and only went out when they had to."

Before Jess could say anything else, Victoria said, "Excuse me while I mingle with our guests." Then she was gone.

Jess finished off her wine as she scanned the crowd. She heard laughter coming from a woman leaning in to hug Daniel. Peter walked up behind Jess and handed her a glass of champagne.

"Should we mingle?" he asked.

"We should," Jess replied, as she linked her arm through his.

Peter led Jess towards a tall, very clean-cut, dark-haired man.

"Leo, I'd like you to meet my wife, Jess. Honey, this is the county's district attorney."

He held out a hand and shook Jess's. "It's a pleasure to meet you."

They chatted for a while and Jess began to feel more at ease. The champagne was beginning to relax her. Peter led her around, introducing her to people he had met since he'd opened his office in town. Eventually, Daniel and Victoria made their way back around to them.

Jess took in her surroundings. "Victoria, the landscaping around your yard is absolutely beautiful. Did you do it yourself?

Victoria laughed. "Oh god no, my store keeps me busy. I couldn't imagine keeping up with all of this, too. Actually, this is Daniel's doing. He calls it his hobby, but I think it's much more than that. I think it's his obsession."

They all laughed.

"We actually met back in college when we were both majoring in botany. I stuck with it, and he switched to horticulture."

Jess studied Daniel. "You studied horticulture, but you're in sales?"

Daniel looked at Jess and said, "That's right."

There was no other explanation, no follow-up. It made Jess feel as though she was somehow intruding into his personal life.

A short, older man wearing aviator's sunglasses had his arm around a woman a little taller than him. The couple strolled over to Daniel and Victoria, and Jess felt a sigh of relief. She hated it when Daniel's steely eyes bore into hers.

The man spoke first. "I hate to interrupt, but we have to be going. As always, it was a great time. Thanks for inviting us."

Daniel shook the man's hand and slapped him on the back. "Thanks for coming. By the way, I don't know if you've met our newest residents, Jess and Peter Stanton. They bought the house next door." He turned to Jess and Peter. "This is David and his wife, Sandra. David is the local sheriff, and Sandra helps Victoria out at the store when she gets busy."

Peter extended a hand. "It's nice to meet you both." He nodded towards David. "I'm sure we'll be seeing a lot of each other. I just opened up a law office on Main Street."

David smiled. "I noticed someone occupied that space. I'm glad to meet you."

He turned to his wife. "Well, Sandra, are you ready?"

She nodded, and they all said their goodbyes.

Jess looked at her watch and said, “We should be going too. I have to let Sampson out.”

“Who’s Sampson?” Victoria asked.

Jess beamed. “Sampson is our newest edition. He’s a puppy that someone dropped off by our lawn. I didn’t have the heart to get rid of him.”

Victoria placed her hands over her heart. “Oh, how nice. I’d love to see him one of these days.”

Jess replied, “I’ll bring him by. Well, thanks for inviting us. We had a wonderful time. Everyone is so nice.”

Jess and Peter turned and walked hand-in-hand back towards their house.

****

That night, Sampson walked over to Jess’s side of the bed and whined. Jess was trying to rouse herself out of a deep sleep when she heard the sound of liquid trickling on the floor. She shot out of bed and grabbed the pup.

“NO, NO, NO,” she whispered in panic as she raced to the door with Sampson. By the time they were outside, Sampson was finished doing his business. Jess continued to watch him sniff around. She wished she’d brought a flashlight with her. It was so dark here in the country. Luckily, there was a full moon, so she had some light to see by.

Her head turned as she heard a vehicle slowly coming down the road and turning into Daniel's driveway. It was odd that the headlights were turned off. She looked at her watch. It was 12:10 a.m. *Awfully late for company, isn't it, Daniel?* she thought to herself. A dark box truck was slowly rolling towards Daniel's house. She thought about running inside and dialing 9-1-1, but would feel foolish if it wasn't a robbery. Instead, she hid behind a tree and watched.

The shadow of a man stepped out onto the driveway, and bright motion lights flicked on. Looking at his stance, Jess was sure it was Daniel. She felt relieved that it wasn't a robbery.

He stood there as the truck drove slowly past him and up to the barn. The doors slid open, and a bright light illuminated the outdoors. Once again, two men dressed in dark clothes opened their doors and unloaded what looked like a couple of mid-sized cardboard boxes; then they handed Daniel a medium sized duffel bag. He unzipped the bag, sifted through the contents, and then nodded. The two men stood outside and talked for a few minutes before driving away.

Jess watched as Daniel turned off the lights, then shut and locked the barn doors. She felt uneasy. Something wasn't right. *Who does this?*

She looked down and saw that Sampson was curled in a ball, sleeping on the grass. With a heavy sigh she picked up the pup and walked into the house, closing the door behind her. Sampson waddled into the bedroom and curled back up on his bed in the corner. Jess groaned at the trail that Sampson had left when she had raced to the door. She grabbed the paper towels and began to clean up the mess. Then she filled a bucket with soapy water and mopped the floor.

Jess looked at her watch. It was only 1:30 a.m. She stifled a yawn and put the mop away. Walking back into her bedroom, she looked at her husband, who hadn't stirred in all the excitement, and shook her head in disbelief.

Jess walked over to the desk in the foyer and pulled out a notebook. She opened it and wrote down the date and time. She made a note of when she saw the box truck and noted the duffel bag being handed off. She made a list of questions after it. *What is in the trucks? What is in the duffel bag? Why are the deliveries so late at night? What is in the shed?*

She yawned again and slipped the notebook back into the drawer. The note she found wedged in the drawer caught her eye. Jess pulled it out again and studied the handwriting. It didn't look like a kid had written it, but what did she know. She didn't have kids and she and her brother had never written notes like that. Could it have been like Peter had said, just a harmless note that meant nothing, or was it a warning? Did someone feel like their life was threatened? She slid it back into the desk and walked back to the bedroom.

She crawled into bed but couldn't sleep. Thoughts of Daniel kept running through her mind. She pictured the man with the scarred face leering at her when he went past. *What's with the box trucks?* she wondered. She really wanted to know what was in that barn. Maybe it was drugs? Or guns? Maybe he ran a human trafficking ring? Whatever it was, Jess had an uneasy feeling about it. She tossed and turned for what felt like hours before finally drifting off to sleep.

****

The blare of the alarm was what she heard first, followed by Peter puttering around in the kitchen, presumably making his morning coffee.

He stepped into the bedroom and asked, "Are you sick?"

"No, why?" she asked, pushing her hair back.

"You never sleep all the way to your alarm unless you're sick."

Jess sighed. "I couldn't sleep."

"What kept you up?" Peter asked.

Jess groaned. "Daniel."

"Daniel?" Peter repeated.

"Yes, Daniel. I took Sampson outside, and there was a box truck that stopped at Daniel's house and unloaded something in his barn."

Peter snorted. "And that kept you awake?"

Jess sat up, irritated. "Not just that. It's every day, Peter, multiple times a day. There's something going on over there."

"Jess, you're sounding like a stalker."

"I'm telling you, Peter, something isn't right."

Peter looked at her, arms crossed. "Something is definitely not right. You are outside in the middle of the night stalking our neighbors. Now you're telling me you're stalking them during the day."

Jess couldn't believe what she was hearing. "I'm not a stalker! I was outside with the dog. She climbed out of bed and started to get dressed in her running clothes.

Peter looked at his watch. "Didn't you say you had a meeting first thing this morning?"

Jess looked down at what she was wearing and groaned. She started to change into a work shirt, thankful that the meeting would be from home.

"I'm telling you, something's not right."

Peter sat down on the edge of the bed and took her hands in his. "I know this move hasn't been easy for you, but you can't start thinking the worst of people. Daniel has been nothing but kind to us. He welcomed us with open arms, and we just went to a party that *he* invited us to. Does that really sound like someone who's doing something illegal? Trust me, honey, guys who do illegal acts want anonymity, not drawing attention to themselves and inviting their neighbors over."

She bit her lower lip, thinking about what he said. "You're right, it doesn't make sense. I don't know what's gotten into me. Can you explain all of the box trucks at his house at all hours of the day and night?"

"Maybe they're deliveries for Victoria's shop? You said he was in sales. Maybe they're deliveries for his clients. There are so many reasonable answers here."

She let out a pent-up breath. "That makes sense. I'm sorry I'm so crazy. It's just so different living here. When you're at work, at least you're around people. The only people I see these days are reflected in a computer screen. Apparently the only other thing I have is an overactive imagination."

Peter leaned over and kissed her. "Please tell me that you'll stop stalking the neighbors."

Jess chuckled. "When you say it like that, I sound like a crazy person. Fine, I'll mind my own business."

He looked at his watch. "I've got to go, or I'll be late. I have an appointment with a client." He put his hand alongside her face and kissed her gently. "It's going to be alright, Jess. Give it time. Maybe drive into town today and visit with Victoria. That might make you feel better about who we're living next to."

Jess gave a sad smile and murmured, "Maybe I'll do that, but first I've got a meeting to attend."

Peter stood up and picked up his briefcase. He slowly walked to the door, and then turned around.

"Are you going to be alright living here? I know I surprised you with the house, but if you don't like it, we can look for something else."

Jess shook her head. "No, that's alright. It's just going to take some getting used to."

Sampson stirred. She walked over and picked him up, nuzzling his nose. "If it weren't for this house, we wouldn't have found Sampson. You're right. I'm overreacting. What you said makes perfect sense. It's probably just deliveries for his sales or the store. I'm being ridiculous."

Peter smiled. "I love you."

She sauntered over to him and kissed him. "I love you, too."

He shut the door behind him, got into his truck, and drove away.

Chapter 7

Jess leashed up Sampson and drove into town. It was hard to believe that it had already been two months since she had moved. The summer heat was beginning to ebb away as fall quietly crept in. The cooler temperatures were a welcome change for Jess and Sampson, and although the pup was quickly growing into a dog, he still had the energy and playfulness of a puppy.

They walked past Walker's General Store, Oliver's Pizza, and then arrived at The Blooming Boutique. Jess admired the colorful bouquets carefully placed in light-colored wicker baskets placed next to the door. Along the front of the store were green striped rain boots bursting with red and yellow tulips. She admired the black iron-framed table adorned with floral mosaic tiles. In the middle of the table sat a red metal truck with the back filled with an arrangement of zinnias, dahlias, and colorful berries. On each chair sat a planter bursting at the seams with yellow and orange mums. Green foliage wrapped around the table stand and snaked along the bottom of the windowsill.

Victoria stepped out of the little shop and smiled at Jess.

"Hi Jess, it's nice to see you." She looked down at Sampson and said, "I see you have Sampson with you today." She reached out and let the dog sniff her hand.

Sampson wagged his tail and placed his head under her hand, letting her pet him between the ears. She knelt down next to him and gave him a good scratch.

"Yes, we needed to get out of the house," Jess replied. She looked around. "Your plants are beautiful."

"Thank you. It's very gratifying. Are you looking for anything in particular?"

"I wasn't, and I don't have a green thumb like you, but I'd love to start designing and landscaping the yard before the weather turns cold. Could you help me with that?"

Victoria smiled. "I have a landscaper on retainer that I can contact for you. He does great work."

"I'd like that," Jess replied.

"Come on in and I'll take down your information."

Both women stepped inside the shop. The smell of scented candles and fresh flowers permeated the space. A small table and chair sat in front of a large window.

"Have a seat and I'll bring us over some coffee."

Jess sat, and Sampson lay down on the floor and was soon fast asleep. Jess looked around the room at the brightly colored bouquets of flowers that filled the coolers. It reminded Jess of the first night they moved into the house. The soft sound of classic rock flowed from speakers near the ceiling.

Victoria carried over a tray with two mugs of coffee, along with a pitcher of milk and a small container of sugar. The coffee tasted heavenly.

Victoria clicked on her pen and started to write down Jess's information.

"Can I ask you a question before we go any farther?" Jess asked.

"Sure," replied Victoria.

Jess gave a nervous laugh, "You're going to think this is crazy, but your landscaper doesn't happen to have a scar down the side of his face, does he?"

Victoria furrowed her brow. "No, he doesn't. He's in his mid-thirties, tall, extremely tan, with short blond hair."

Jess breathed out a sigh of relief. "Good. No offense, but the guy with the scar down his face gave me the creeps as he drove past me when I was jogging last month."

"Why would you think that guy was my landscaper?" Victoria asked.

"Well, for starters, he pulled out of your driveway. He was driving a box truck." Jess explained.

A brief look of trepidation passed over Victoria's face. "Oh, it must have been a delivery. You know Daniel is in sales. He gets a lot of deliveries."

Before Jess had a chance to respond, Victoria looked down at her notebook. "What's a good number to reach you?"

Jess got the hint to change the subject, and answered the rest of Victoria's questions. Sampson began to stir, and Jess looked down at him, then over to Victoria.

"I would love to buy a plant." Jess said smiling at Victoria. "What would you suggest?"

Victoria walked over and picked up a cute tin planter with azaleas and handed it to Jess. "There are directions for their care on the card that's tucked in the planter. If you have any questions, you know where I live."

They both laughed.

"Well, I should take this lug outside," Jess said, once she had paid "Thank you for all of your help, and I can't wait to meet your landscaper."

"You're welcome. I'm sure he will transform your space into the yard of your dreams."

Jess walked outside with Sampson. The sun was shining, and the temperature had risen. She took off her plaid flannel shirt, revealing her white tank top, and wrapped the shirt around her waist. She liked Victoria, but she couldn't shake the feeling that Daniel was another story. She wondered about the odd look that passed over Victoria's face when she mentioned the man with the scar. There was more to this story, and she was going to find out what it was.

She continued walking towards Peter's office. She walked past Oliver's Pizza, and the smell of pizza made her stomach growl. She was tempted to stop but kept walking. Maybe she could tempt Peter into going to lunch with her.

When she arrived, she was disappointed to see that the office was locked up, and no one was there. A plastic clock signaled that he'd be back by two o'clock. Jess looked at her watch. It was eleven-thirty. She didn't want to wait around. She looked down at Sampson. "Well, boy, should we go home?"

The car was down the road across from the park. She tugged at the leash and quickly crossed the street.

As she drove past Daniel's house, she spotted a box truck again, and the door to the barn was open. Daniel hadn't spotted her yet, so she craned her neck trying to see inside. The light was on, and from a distance, there were lines of buckets with plants of varying heights. On the other side were what appeared to be 3 people carrying boxes and putting them into the truck.

Her heart skipped a beat when she noticed Daniel staring at her. He must have said something to the two guys who were standing next to him, because they both turned and looked at her. One of them was the man with the scar down his face. Her heart sank, and she quickly turned her head away and continued home.

When she walked inside the house, she locked the door. She knew she wasn't crazy. That man gave her the creeps. Something wasn't right. Jess knew in her gut that Daniel was doing something illegal. He had to be. She didn't know what kind of plants were inside the barn, but she had a good idea. You didn't have men driving to the house multiple times daily dropping off duffel bags and who knows what else unless something shady was going on.

Jess walked to the desk and pulled out her notebook. She grabbed a pen and wrote down what she had seen. She knew she'd need more proof than a notebook noting the times of deliveries and observations she'd seen, but it was a start.

She jumped when she heard a loud shot ring out. It sounded like a gun. She had never been around guns when she lived in the city. The only gunfire she had seen or heard had always been on television. She looked out her window and saw the two goons, Scar-face and a shorter stocky man, shooting at targets towards the back of Daniel's yard.

She couldn't stop shaking as she stood and watched the men. They were laughing as they aimed their pistols, piercing the target.

Sampson started barking. She looked at him in panic. "Sampson, NO!" she yelled, but that just made him bark more.

She looked back out the window and saw the man with the scar down his face turning and looking at her. He grinned and pointed his pistol at her. She screamed and quickly ran from the window. She heard another gunshot, but it wasn't in her direction. If it were, she was sure she'd hear glass shattering. Her hands were shaking as she hastily grabbed her keys and the leash. She ran to her car, hoping they wouldn't see her, and fled out of the driveway.

****

As Jess drove away, Daniel shook his head and clapped his hand on the man's shoulder.

The shorter, stockier man looked at Daniel. "I think we got our point across, boss. What do you think?"

Daniel smiled and pulled out a cigar. He lit it and inhaled. After he exhaled a puff of smoke he responded. "I think she got the message."

He looked from one man to the other. "See boys, sometimes a little message is all it takes to help someone see reason. Once she stops sticking her nose in other people's business. She'll come around, everyone does. She just needs to understand how things are done in this town, that's all."

The two men with Daniel smiled. Daniel took one last look at the Stantons' house, then turned and walked away. This was his town and he refused to hide from some uppity busybody.

****

Jess drove straight to the police station and walked inside, with Sampson by her side. She had finally stopped shaking and was now enraged. She saw David, the sheriff.

"Hi, David. I don't know if you remember me."

David looked up from his desk and smiled. "Of course I do, Jess. How are you?"

She could feel herself relax and cleared her throat. "I know this sounds crazy, but please, just hear me out."

"Alright," David said studying her carefully. "Why don't you have a seat and tell me what's going on."

Jess sat down across from him.

"I think…no, I'm positive that Daniel is doing something illegal. I'm pretty sure it's drugs."

"He's doing drugs?" David asked confused.

Jess shook her head. "No, he's growing and dealing drugs."

David leaned forward and folded his hands together. "Jess, that's quite an accusation. I've known Daniel going on twenty years and I can tell you with certainty he's a solid, upstanding member of this community."

Jess raised her hands in a stopping motion. "Please, just hear me out. Every day, multiple times a day, there are these box trucks driving in and out of his place. Each time, the driver gives him a black duffel bag." She put up a hand to stop the sheriff from interrupting. "He keeps everything in his barn. Today, I drove past and saw part of what's in the barn. There were plants of varying heights and people working at a table on the other side."

David was quiet as Jess continued, "Daniel saw me looking, so he knows that I saw. That's when the gunfire started."

David leaned back, startled. "Daniel shot at you?"

Jess stood up and paced with panic in her voice. "Not exactly at me. His goons were shooting targets in the backyard. I looked out my window, and one of the men pointed the gun right at me. I believe it was a warning for me to stay away."

A look of understanding crossed David's face. "Do you have any proof of this?"

"No, but I know what I saw."

"I'm not saying that I don't believe you, but without proof, I can't do anything about it. It's your word against his."

"Unbelievable," Jess muttered.

"Does Peter know about this?"

Jess shook her head no.

David folded his hands together on his desk and held her eyes with his. "So, what you're saying is that Daniel has deliveries to his house which are deposited in his barn. His wife owns a greenhouse and there are plants in the barn. He's also in sales and does business with pretty much everyone in town. He receives a duffel bag, did you say?" He didn't wait for her to answer. "Well, there's no crime in that, and as for the shooting, that isn't against the law, either. People do that here, what with all the wildlife around here-- and to be honest, some people just like to shoot."

Jess sat in disbelief. "My house is right next to his. Surely, there's some kind of distance law."

David laughed sarcastically. "Jess, I've seen where your house is. You are plenty far away. Let me give you a piece of advice. You just moved here, so listen closely. You can't go around accusing people of things that they didn't do. That is called a rumor, and people don't take kindly to rumors, especially from people who don't know what they're talking about. Go home, Jess, and please, mind your own business and stay out of Daniel's. Like I said, he's a solid upstanding citizen, and you won't find a better neighbor. For your sake, let's just keep this conversation between us. It'll be better that way."

Jess couldn't believe what she was hearing. Worst of all, what he had said was right. She had no definite proof. She would have to fix that. She would show David that she was right. Daniel was not the solid, upstanding citizen that this town thought he was.

****

That night at dinner, Peter asked, "How was your day?"

Jess faked a smile and said, "It was fine. I drove into town and stopped at The Blooming Boutique. Victoria's plants are beautiful. We started talking and I set up an appointment to meet with a landscaper."

Peter looked at her with pleasure. "That's great news. Once you make this place your own, I think you will like it better."

Jess picked up her water and took a sip.

"I saw David today," continued Peter.

Jess interrupted, "I knew he couldn't keep his mouth shut. After he lectured me about not saying anything!"

"What are you talking about?" Peter asked.

"What are *you* talking about?" Jess asked, feeling like she had opened mouth and inserted foot.

Peter put down his fork. "I was going to say that he said to say hi. Now, what do you have to say?"

Jess looked at her husband and knew she couldn't lie to him, no matter what David said. "I had a visit with him this afternoon."

"Oh, he didn't mention it," Peter commented, going back to cutting his steak.

Jess cleared her throat. "I know, now. I wouldn't have gone to him if I didn't think a bullet was going to come through the window."

"What!" Peter exclaimed. "What bullet? What happened?"

Jess took a sip of her water. "Yes! So, I reported it to David, who said it's not illegal to shoot on your own property and our house is far enough away. Then I told him about all the box truck deliveries, the plants in the barn--"

Peter stood up. "Please tell me you're joking! Jess, you can't go around making accusations. Do you realize how crazy you sound? These are our neighbors. They have shown us nothing but kindness. You sound like a stalker."

She turned her back and started running water in the sink without saying anything. Peter walked over to her and turned off the water. He put his hands on her shoulders and turned her towards him. "Didn't we just talk about this? Are you stupid?"

His voice was beginning to rise as he started pacing the kitchen, flailing his arms. "I'm trying to start a business in this town. I need to earn these people's trust. I can't do that if you're starting rumors about Daniel!"

Her eyes filled with tears. She knew realistically that he was right. She didn't have proof about the man pointing the gun, and she didn't have proof of Daniel doing anything illegal. Maybe she was being stupid. She should have known better, but the goons shooting guns really terrified her.

"I'm sorry. I wasn't thinking," she whispered. "I saw them shooting guns and I panicked."

"We live in the country. It's going to happen. People have more freedom to do things here, including shooting a gun." He stopped pacing and looked at her. "I don't know what else to do here, Jess. Do you want me to talk to Daniel? Would that make you stop this crazy paranoia?"

Now he was making her feel foolish. She hated that about him. "No, it's fine. It's just another thing that I have to get used to. Life is just different here, that's all."

Peter shook his head. "Unbelievable," he muttered, and walked out of the kitchen.

A few seconds later, she heard the door to his office slam shut. She knew she appeared paranoid, and maybe even a little bit crazy, but she remembered Victoria's expression when she mentioned the man with the scar. She knew the box truck deliveries day-in, and day-out weren't legal deliveries. She was going to find out what was really going on, and when she did, Peter would be the one feeling like a fool.

Chapter 8

A couple of weeks later, Jess jogged past the front of Daniel's house. His car wasn't in the driveway, and Jess felt a wave of relief.

Victoria came out the front door and began walking towards the mailbox. She waved at Jess. "Hi Jess, it's nice to see you again."

Jess eased into a slow jog in place. "Hi, Victoria. How are you?"

Victoria smiled sadly. "Tired. It's been a long week and I'm beat."

Jess sympathized. "I know how you feel. Sitting in front of a computer, meeting with clients all day, can be exhausting too. The only thing that seems to help is going for a run."

. "Do you run often?"

"Every chance I get."

Victoria shook her head. "I envy you. I haven't run since I opened up the shop five years ago."

"Well, you're here now. Do you want to go for a run?"

Victoria looked at the sky and seemed to be thinking. "I'd love to. Do you have time for me to change?"

Jess grinned. "Absolutely, I'm in no hurry. Like I said, it's to save my sanity."

Victoria let out a squeal of excitement, then turned and ran into the house. She was back out within minutes. She quickly stretched, and they started off at a comfortable pace.

"This is just what I needed," Victoria said.

Jess looked at her and smiled. "I think I just found my new running partner."

"Sign me up."

They ran in comfortable silence for about a mile before Victoria asked, "Do you have any family around here?"

Jess looked at her, surprised. "No." After a few minutes of more silence, she said, "Why do you ask?"

Victoria laughed. "I asked because we don't get many people relocating and opening up a business in our tiny town. I was just curious. Forget I asked."

Jess pointed to a log sitting beside the creek. They slowed to a walk and sat down, watching the water flow downstream.

Jess picked up a rock and tossed it into the water. "We moved here because Peter got tired of working nonstop at the law firm. He wanted his own law office so he could make his own hours. He happened to see the law office in town for rent. He started looking at houses in the area and bought the house we're in for our anniversary."

"Wow, that's some anniversary gift! How long have you been married?"

Jess laughed. "One year. I told him it was a little excessive."

"Well, now that you've been here for a couple of months how are you adjusting to our little corner of the world?"

Jess quietly pondered how honest she wanted to be. "I love drinking coffee on my porch in the morning before I start work, and I'm starting to enjoy the peace and quiet." She thought of Daniel, faked a giggle, and lied, "My neighbors are the best. I would say I'm enjoying life."

Victoria chuckled. "This place really grows on you. I'm really glad you're adjusting. I'd hate it if you moved."

They got up and started to run towards home.

When they reached the house, Victoria asked, "Do you want to get together for lunch one day this week?"

"I'd love to," Jess replied. "I'll check my schedule and let you know."

****

A few days later, Jess sat at her computer finishing up a report for work. She stood up and stretched. "Sampson!" Jess called. Sampson didn't appear. *Where could he have gone to this time?* she thought. She walked into the bedroom and looked at his bed. He wasn't there.

"Sampson!" She shouted again. *Where are you?* As she entered the kitchen, she saw his food and water dish were untouched. She groaned when she spotted the kitchen door wide open. "Sampson!" There was still no sign of him. Jess could feel her heart pounding in her chest.

She walked over to Daniel's house and knocked on the door. Daniel answered the door and smiled at Jess. "Hi, Jess. Are you looking for Sampson?"

"Actually, I am. Have you seen him?"

"He's in the yard. I found him wandering on the road in front of the house. I tied him up out back to keep him safe until I had time to bring him back to your house."

Jess walked around to the back of the house and was relieved to see Sampson. He was lying on the grass with his eyes closed. Jess thought it was strange that he wasn't jumping up to greet her.

She knelt down to pet him. He yelped when she touched a spot that was tender on his back.

"I suspect he got into a scuffle with a wild animal, but I think he'll be okay," Daniel said.

Sampson stood and slowly wagged his tail. Jess clipped on his leash and looked up at Daniel.

"Thanks, Daniel, for keeping an eye on him for me."

"You're welcome," David replied then he walked back into the house.

****

A few weeks later, Jess stepped into Monique's Diner and saw Victoria sitting at a table looking at her phone.

"Sorry I'm late," Jess said breathlessly sliding into the booth. "Some clients just keep going and going. I didn't think the meeting was ever going to end."

Victoria laughed. "I know what you mean. No worries, I just got here a few minutes ago myself."

The two women ordered their meals and began talking about the ups and downs of business and pleasing clients.

Once their order arrived, Jess changed the subject, "Since your shop is closed tomorrow would you like to go for a run?"

Victoria shook her head. "Sorry, tomorrow is our anniversary. Daniel is taking me away for a couple of days."

"Oh, happy almost anniversary. How long have you been married?"

Victoria finished chewing. "We'll have been married for ten years."

"Ten years is a long time. What's the secret to staying happily married?" Jess asked, truly curious.

Victoria shrugged and thought for a minute. "I guess you just make it work however you can. I mean, it's not always easy staying married, but we make it work."

Jess noticed that Victoria was looking out the window, and she looked sad. It felt like there was more that Victoria wasn't telling her, but she didn't know her well enough to ask. So instead, she said, "Well, I hope Peter and I are lucky enough to endure the ups and downs of marriage like you and Daniel. You two seem happy."

Victoria looked back at her and smiled. "I'm sure you will."

They ate in companionable silence for a few minutes. Jess studied her friend. Victoria was dressed in a long green floral skirt and a jade-colored long sleeve shirt.

The waitress took their plates away and brought them each a cup of coffee. Jess took a sip, then asked, "Aren't you hot in long sleeves? I know it's mid-September, but it's dreadfully hot out today."

Victoria shrugged like it was a question she was asked every day. "I work with thorny plants that scratch up my arms. I like to hide them when I can. Let's quit talking about me. Believe me, I'm a boring subject."

Jess thought for a moment then asked, "What made Daniel switch from horticulture to sales?"

Victoria looked confused at the quick change in conversation. She shrugged, then replied, “He’s always been passionate about both, really. He stuck with horticulture for a long time, then thought it was more practical to move into sales. Believe me, he’s an asset when I need some help or advice with either my plants or my business.”

Victoria quickly switched the conversation back to Jess. It felt to Jess that Victoria wanted to avoid any conversation about Daniel. “So, now that you’ve been here awhile, I’ve got to ask. Are you getting used to country life?”

Jess smiled, remembering when Victoria asked her that same question when they were first getting to know each other. This time, she didn’t feel like she was making up an answer. “I think so. Some days it’s hard to be so far away from my friends and family. I feel so isolated. Then there are other days when it’s hard for me to come inside because it’s so beautiful outside and I can work in the yard, go for a run, and Sampson’s antics always have me laughing. Those are the days when I’m happy where we are, and I wouldn’t trade it for the world.”

Victoria took a sip of her coffee and nodded. “I remember feeling like that myself when Daniel and I moved up here from the city. Believe me, once you start meeting people and learning your way around more, you'll feel right at home."

Once lunch was finished and Victoria paid the bill, the two women exited the diner. Jess turned towards Victoria. "Thanks for lunch, Victoria. Next week, I'll buy."

Victoria laughed. "I'll you hold you to it." She looked at her watch. "I have to get back to work, but maybe we can go for a run later this week?

Jess smiled. "I'd love to. Thanks for the company. I don't know what I would do without you here to keep me sane."

The two women laughed as Victoria turned and started walking to The Blooming Boutique, and Jess walked to her car to begin the drive home.

When she turned left onto her road, she was thinking about her lunch with Victoria. Over the past few weeks, they had really begun to bond. She couldn't imagine Victoria staying with someone unscrupulous. Maybe he was just getting deliveries. It didn't sound as though he was doing anything illegal the way Victoria acted. He sounded like a husband who supported his wife.

She really wanted to believe that. She really wanted to believe that Daniel wasn't up to no good, that he really was on the up-and-up, but she couldn't. Her intuition told her otherwise and she always trusted her intuition.

She drove past Daniel's house and saw him outside watering the plants. She pulled into their driveway and parked the car. She got out and walked towards him. He didn't look thrilled, but quickly covered it up with a huge grin that Jess knew was fake. Maybe he just didn't like people, she surmised. She was going to give him the benefit of the doubt. She almost lost her nerve, but quickly steeled herself, thinking that two could play the fake game.

"Hi, Daniel. It's a lovely day out today, isn't it?"

Daniel looked at her and replied, "That it is. What can I do for you, Jess?"

Jess thought quickly. "I was hoping you could give me a recommendation. I need to have some work done on my car. Where would you suggest?"

Daniel opened his mouth to speak just as a box truck began to drive down the driveway. Jess couldn't help herself. Here was her chance to see inside the barn. She had him. She would finally have proof.

Daniel shook his head, "I'm sorry, Jess, but I've got some work to do. We use Matt's Garage for all our automobile needs. He's reasonable and reliable."

Daniel started walking towards the truck. Jess followed, determined to see what was in the barn, or at least in all of these box trucks.

The man with the scar on his face hopped out of the truck and the shorter, stocky man exited on the other side. Jess inwardly cringed but was determined to stay. She smiled at the men and stuck her hand out towards the short, stocky one.

"Hi, I'm Jess Stanton."

She looked expectantly at the man, waiting for him to shake her hand and introduce himself. He didn't. Instead, he smiled slyly while openly checking her out and said, "Nice to meet you."

Daniel intervened. "Jess, I've got some work to do. I hate to be rude, but you understand."

She faltered for a brief second before pasting on a smile. "Of course. Well, it was nice meeting you."

She climbed back into her car and drove away, relieved to be gone but frustrated with herself that she couldn't get a look inside the truck or barn. She opened the front door and called for Sampson. He came running down the stairs and out the door, happy to be outside.

She stood nonchalantly, trying not to make it obvious that she was looking over towards Daniel's house. Once again, the men handed off a duffel bag and the truck backed into the barn. From the angle she was standing, she wasn't able to see into the barn. She groaned in frustration. There had to be a way to find out what was in there.

After thinking for a few minutes, Jess finally came up with a plan. "Sampson, come," she whispered. Sampson followed her into the house. He wagged his tail as she gave him a treat. "Stay," she ordered. Jess held the empty leash in her hand and started walking across Daniel's yard, yelling Sampson's name. Her stomach clenched as she braced herself and walked over towards the barn. The man with the scar started to close the door but not before she saw some tall plants with spiky leaves sitting on counters.

The door closed quickly, and one of the men said, "Can I help you?"

Jess tried to look worried. "My dog ran off and I was wondering if he ran over here. Do you think he could have run inside the barn?"

The man stood in front of the barn with his arms crossed. He reminded her of a fortress that would not be moved. "No, your dog is not here. I suggest you move along."

Jess tried to smile. "Do you mind if I take a look? He's quick and maybe he ran in before you closed the doors."

He glared at her without speaking.

She shrugged. "If you happen to see him, can you send him over to my house?"

He still didn't answer her.

She continued the charade of calling for Sampson as she walked back over towards her house.

****

Later that evening, Sampson whined to go outside. Jess grabbed a flashlight on her way out. She still felt ill at ease with how dark it got in, and the sounds of nocturnal animals made her feel uncomfortable. She clicked on the light and stood behind one of the trees, hoping she was out of sight. She looked towards Daniel's house, still hoping she might see something. Instead, Sampson walked over towards the car and sniffed around on the ground.

"Sampson," Jess hissed but he refused to come to her. *What is going on with you,* she thought as she walked over to Sampson. Her heart sank when she saw a flat tire on her rear wheel. She walked inside the house.

"Peter," she yelled.

He came walking downstairs from his office. "What's wrong?"

"I have a flat tire," she grumbled, annoyed. "I must have run over something on my way home."

Peter went back upstairs and changed his clothes. He walked outside and opened the trunk to take out the spare tire and jack. Jess held the flashlight for him so that he could see. It didn't take long for him to change the tire and put the flat one in her trunk.

He looked at her. "Tomorrow, drive into town to a garage and see if they can repair it."

"I'll take it to Matt's Garage in the morning," Jess replied.

He looked at her quizzically. "Matt's Garage?"

Jess looked up at him in surprise and tried to cover her tracks. "Someone had mentioned having some work done at Matt's Garage when we were at Daniel's cookout," she lied.

"Oh," Peter replied. "Well, see if they can fix the tire for you."

The next morning, Jess drove carefully into town, where, thanks to her GPS, she was able to find Matt's Garage. The garage had just opened, so she was the only customer. While she was waiting for her tire to be repaired, she scrolled through her phone.

"Excuse me, ma'am. Are you the one waiting for a tire repair?"

"Yes, I am," she replied. "Were you able to fix it?"

"No, sorry. You have a big slice in your tire. It's bigger than a repair kit can handle. You're going to need a new tire."

Jess groaned. She hadn't expected this. "Do you know what I ran over?"

He shrugged. "No, sorry. It was a clean cut. It's smooth like some sort of blade or something. It's not jagged like a rip from a rock, and it's too big for it to be a nail or screw."

Jess thought back to her visit at Daniel's house and wondered if the problem with the tire was just a coincidence. Did Daniel have something to do with her flat tire?

"I'll purchase a new tire if you have one in stock," Jess said hoping it could be done quickly.

"We should have the new one on in no time."

Half an hour later, Jess was back on the road, heading home. As she passed Daniel's, she didn't stop, even though he was outside working on his lawn. Instead, she looked straight ahead and quickly continued home.

Maybe this was why the former house owners were unfriendly. Maybe they knew something about Daniel that kept them away. Something that Jess was determined to figure out.

Chapter 9

The next week, the doorbell rang. Jess answered the door and came face-to-face with a tanned man with short blond hair. He smiled and held out his hand.

"Mrs. Stanton? We talked on the phone. I'm Mark. I'm the landscaper that Victoria referred you to."

Jess smiled and shook his hand. "Hi Mark and please, call me Jess. I've been expecting you. Come on in."

Mark stepped inside the house and said, "I appreciate your patience. I know it's been about a month, but I've got a very small crew, and we like to finish one job before we start another. This way you get our undivided attention."

Jess shrugged, completely at ease around him. "It's not a problem. I was in no hurry. Would you like something to drink? Lemonade, beer, water?"

He smiled but shook his head. "I don't drink when I'm working, but I'd love a glass of lemonade."

After Jess had filled their glasses, she led him outside to walk around the yard.

"This is such a big yard, and I just don't know what I should do with it. I really need your help."

Mark laughed. "Each yard is different, but I can definitely help you with yours."

They spent the next two hours discussing different kinds of plants and trees that would enhance the look of the yard. They walked over toward the tree line that separated the two properties. Daniel was outside watering his plants. He waved when he saw the two of them.

"I see Victoria referred you to a great landscaper," Daniel said as he walked over and shook hands with Mark.

Mark glanced out across Daniel's yard. "Your yard looks fantastic, Daniel."

"It's a labor of love. You'll have to come over and take a look sometime when you're not busy," Daniel said proudly.

Jess tried to look at ease. "Daniel, you'll have to give me some tips on how to keep my plants looking so beautiful."

Daniel smiled. "That's an easy one. It's all in the watering. Keep them watered, and they'll keep growing. I suppose I should let the two of you get back to business. It was nice seeing you again, Mark."

He went back to watering, and Jess and Mark resumed their tour of the yard. Every so often, Mark would stop and take measurements, or make a quick sketch in his notebook. When he was finished, they climbed back up the steps of the porch and sat down across from each other in the Adirondack chairs.

"Your yard has so many possibilities," Mark began. He pulled out his sketchbook. "Just give me a few minutes to sketch out some ideas and then we'll talk."

While Mark sketched, Jess looked over at Daniel still watering his yard. It seemed that these days he was always out watering, and if Jess didn't know better, watching everything she did.

Mark interrupted her thoughts. "Here's some designs that would look natural in this landscape." He had placed a few more flowerbeds throughout the yard. "You should also have mulch around your trees to keep the moisture in. There's a variety of colors you can choose from." Mark reached into his briefcase and pulled out some albums showcasing different mulch types.

They spent the next hour discussing borders and plant types. When they were finished and Mark had a starting point, he stood up to leave.

Jess stopped him. "Mark, can I ask you something?"

"Sure." He sat back down.

Jess thought back to the note she found in the kitchen drawer. "Did you happen to meet the people who owned this house while you were working next door?"

"Actually, I did. They were very nice people. They were a young couple. It was the first house that they had owned. They had a lot of ideas for renovating the place, and after seeing it for myself, they did a beautiful job."

Jess was astonished at hearing something nice about the mysterious couple. "Can you tell me anything else about them? I have some questions about the house and wanted to contact them, but I can't seem to find their number or email address. I've asked around, but no one seems to know how to contact them."

Mark shook his head. "Sorry, I can't help you there. Maybe Daniel or Victoria might have something that can help you. Chad was always hanging out at Daniel's place. Sometimes they'd go golfing or the four of them would meet up at Daniel's house and go out somewhere together. The four of them were inseparable for a while."

This was a surprise to Jess. "I asked Daniel and Victoria about the Wellingtons once, but I was told that they were an odd couple and not very friendly. It sounds like maybe they had a falling out."

Mark rubbed the back of his neck. "I never quite understood what happened. It just seemed like overnight they were all friends and then they weren't. You know, now that I think of it, I once overheard Daniel ask Chad…never mind. It's none of my business, and I respect my clients' privacy. Forget I said anything."

Jess switched tactics. "I appreciate that you respect your clients' privacy, I really do, but Mark, were Chad and his wife ever in danger?"

"Danger? Why would they be in danger?"

Jess looked pointedly at him. "You said they weren't friends anymore, so I'm asking if they were in danger?"

Mark ran his hands through his hair. "I don't know what happens in the city when you don't agree with someone, but it doesn't mean that person is in danger."

Jess was silent. Maybe she shouldn't have said anything. This wasn't going as she had planned. "I apologize, Mark. I must sound a little crazy."

Mark's face was a blank page. "Like I said, Mrs. Stanton, I really don't know about the comings and goings of my clients. If things were reversed, you wouldn't want me to be blabbing around town about your business, so respect me when I say to give Daniel the same courtesy."

He stood up, indicating he was ready to leave.

Jess shot him one more question: "How long did this disagreement happen before they put their house up for sale?"

Mark smiled coyly. "Who said they had a disagreement? Now you're just putting words in my mouth." He looked down at the sketchbook in his hand. "I should be ready to start in about a week. Does that work for you?"

Jess knew better than to push her luck. "That's perfect. Thank you, Mark, for all of your help."

"You're welcome." He hesitated for a minute, and then said, "Let me give you a piece of advice, and I hope you don't take it the wrong way. Small towns protect their own. Poking around in another person's business doesn't bode well."

Jess blew out a long breath. "I'm sorry. I'm not looking for trouble. It's just that the Wellingtons lived in this house, and no one seems to know much about them. I think it's odd no one knows how to contact them or know why they just instantly disappeared." She drew in a deep breath, and then exhaled. "On the other hand, I know you're right. I should just mind my own business. Thanks again for all of your help."

"You're welcome." He looked over at Daniel's house, then back at Jess. He sat back down.

"Have you seen the park in the middle of town? The one with the basketball courts and skateboard ramps?"

Jess nodded. "I have. It's well-maintained and seems to get a lot of use."

"It does. Did you know that Daniel helped to fund most of that?"

Jess shook her head no.

"The flowers hanging from the lampposts? Those are donated by Victoria."

Jess felt chagrined. "They're beautiful."

"They are. Have you noticed that we don't have a lot of 'big box stores' but instead we have small, local businesses?"

Jess felt even smaller. "Let me guess… Daniel is responsible for that too?"

Mark crossed his arms. "Yep. You see Daniel believes in local business. Our town runs smoothly. If someone is struggling, he's the first to help out. Everyone in this town wants to see the other person succeed. It works."

"It seems as though Daniel runs this town," Jess observed.

"Nope, quite the opposite. Daniel doesn't hold a seat or position in this town. He works behind the scenes. He makes himself available. There's no one else who works harder for this town than he does."

Jess couldn't help herself; the words were out before she could think better of them. "What does Daniel get in return?"

Mark shrugged. "A great town. A town where business is thriving. Great schools. Why is it so hard to see the good in people, Jess?"

Jess had no response. She wanted to say, *His behavior is bizarre.* Her intuition was screaming that there was something going on. The note that was stuck in the back of the drawer that someone felt they were in danger. The spiky plants littering his shed. Instead, she cleared her throat and said, "I'm sorry. I guess my imagination was working overtime. I blame it on the seclusion."

Jess stood up as Mark started down the stairs. She couldn't help herself, she blurted out, "How can you explain all the box trucks coming in and out at all hours of the day and night?"

Mark shrugged and said, "I don't have to. It's none of my business."

Chapter 10

Jess walked into The Booming Boutique and was surprised at how busy the little shop was. There were people milling around the store, and also a line in front of the cash register. Victoria was smiling at the customers, but Jess could tell that she looked a little stressed. She made a beeline to the counter.

"Would you like some help?" Jess asked Victoria.

Victoria looked at her friend gratefully. "I'd love some. Do you know anything about plants?"

"Umm, no," laughed Jess. "But I do know how to run a cash register. Do you want to trade places?"

Victoria moved away from the cash register and let Jess slide in. Victoria walked over to the people admiring some of her planters. Jess smiled and rang up the next customer.

Half an hour later, the store was cleared out. Both women, exhausted, sat down at the small table in front of the window.

Victoria pushed her hair out of the eyes. "Thanks for helping. I don't know what I would have done without you."

Jess shrugged. "You would have managed." She stood up and walked over to the coffee bar and filled two mugs with coffee. She carried them over, knowing that Victoria liked her coffee black.

"Did someone call in sick?" Jess asked.

"No. Someone quit, and I thought I could manage without hiring a replacement. Obviously, that was a mistake."

"Do you need someone full time?" Jess asked, taking a sip of coffee.

"No, that's why I thought I could get away without hiring someone else. I just need someone two days a week. One day when I get deliveries, and days when I have an event going on, like a wedding for example."

"I could do it," Jess replied.

"Really?"

"Sure, it would be fun. Honestly, I look around this shop and feel inspired. You've created so many beautiful things. I'd like to learn more about plants. Maybe it'll help me keep the ones I have at home alive," she said, laughing.

"You're hired," Victoria said excitedly. "What brought you here today anyway? Did you just stop to say hi?"

Jess laughed. "Actually, no. I wanted to thank you for recommending Mark to landscape the yard. He came up with some great ideas."

"I'm really glad it's going to work out."

As the two women sipped their coffee's, Peter walked into the shop. His eyes widened when he saw Jess sitting at the table. "What are you doing here?"

"I stopped to see Victoria. What are you doing here?"

He smiled and leaned down. "Close your eyes and pretend to be surprised."

Jess did as she was told.

Peter walked over and picked up a bouquet of red roses. He walked to the counter, and Victoria rang him up.

"Open your eyes." Peter said tenderly.

Her hand went over her mouth. "Oh Peter, they're beautiful!"

"What's the occasion?" Victoria asked with a grin.

Peter handed the bouquet to Jess and said, "Today is my wife's birthday. Happy birthday."

Victoria jumped up. "You didn't tell me it was your birthday."

"I didn't want to make a big deal about it."

Peter looked at his wife. "Would you like to go to lunch since you're in town?"

"Oliver's Pizza?" Jess asked hopefully.

"The best pizza in town," Victoria chimed in.

Peter held out his hand and pulled Jess up.

“Bye, Victoria. Call me when you want me to come in.”

“You got it. Now, get out of here and enjoy your birthday.”

****

Sampson whined and nudged Jess’s hand to wake her up. She looked at the clock. It was one fifteen in the morning. She slipped on her jeans, t-shirt, and running shoes. She grabbed his leash and Sampson led her outside. It was cooler out at night, and she rubbed her arms trying to warm up.

She looked up at the moon. She thought about how much her life had changed since she moved up here. She and Victoria were getting closer, and it was nice to have a friend again. It made her feel more settled. She was looking forward to helping Victoria out at The Blooming Boutique.

She smiled as she watched Sampson sniffing around in the yard. She loved having a dog around. It reminded her of her brother, Jason, and the German Shephard they used to own. That dog would follow Jason everywhere. She missed him. She would have loved to talk to him about how she was feeling about Daniel. She was confused. What if she found out that Daniel really was some sort of drug dealer?

How would that affect Victoria and her shop? How could she do that to someone who was beginning to become a good friend?

On the other hand, if Daniel was a drug dealer, how could she not *do* anything? A drug dealer had in essence killed her brother by supplying him; how could she not try to save another person's loved one? She couldn't in good conscience let it go. She hoped she was wrong, and Daniel wasn't this awful man doing awful things. She needed to be sure.

Once Sampson was finished, she led him across the lawn and into the back of Daniel's yard. She stuck to the outer edges, although by looking at Daniel's dark house, she was confident that she would not be caught trespassing.

Her heart was pounding in her chest as she made her way to the barn. She stopped at the edge of the barn, and for a brief moment, wondered if she was doing the right thing. She wanted answers, but she wasn't sure she wanted to break the law to get them. She thought of David and knew the police would be no help. Peter would go ballistic if he knew what she was up to. She didn't have a choice. It was now or never. She could do this on her own. She had to.

Jess put her hand on the wooden handle and groaned when she saw the padlock on the door. *Great,* she thought. Wiggling the padlock, she discovered that it wasn't completely pushed down. She lifted the lock and twisted it, opening the door. It was dark as she quickly pulled Sampson into the barn and shut the door. Jess turned on the flashlight of her cell phone and tried to see the layout of the shed.

She walked over towards the side wall, to a long counter filled with different chemicals and snapped a picture. The flash went off as she quickly snapped picture after picture of tables topped with a variety of glass bottles, heat-safe dishes, rubber tubing, and stacks of cheesecloth. Another table was filled with cylinders labeled "hcl". Jess didn't know what the letters meant, but she would look it up at home. Time was of the essence, and she was not going to waste any time while she was here. Along one of the walls were steel drums that weren't labeled. As she continued to click pictures, she saw stoves and cooking pots that she was sure were used for making meth.

She clicked off her phone and slid it into her back pocket.

Sampson started barking.

"Shh, Sampson, NO," she hissed.

She tugged at Sampson and grabbed the handle to slide open the door. It was locked. She tried pushing harder and panicked when the door wouldn't budge. She thought of calling Peter, but she didn't want to fight again. With these pictures, she could prove that he was dealing in illegal drug activities.

She looked around, panicked. Daniel or whoever locked her in here couldn't find her phone. That would end in disaster. She couldn't let them find it on her, and she couldn't let them find it lying somewhere in the barn. She turned off the phone and slid it into her bra. She tried to remain calm and turned her head to see if there were any windows that she could climb out of. There weren't, and with her phone turned off, it was too dark to see around the barn.

She sat with Sampson, feeling defeated. Whoever locked her in here wasn't in a hurry to confront her. She reached under her shirt to pull out her phone. She had no other choice but to call Peter. She'd be damned if she was going to stay here any longer.

Just as she started to punch in the numbers, she heard the click of the door being unlocked. She quickly slid her phone down inside the front of her pants. She pulled her hand out as the door opened.

The moon was full letting in some light and her heart sank when she saw a dark silhouetted figure standing in the doorway. The light clicked on and she squinted her eyes. There, stood Daniel.

"Jess, this is a surprise. What are you doing here?" his voice was calm, but she could see the anger in his eyes.

She cleared her throat. "I… uh… what I mean to say is, Sampson needed to go out and I had taken the leash off him. Unfortunately, he took off and ran over here. I noticed the door was open and I went in to look for Samson. As you can see, I found him."

Daniel looked at her and said nothing. Jess knew he didn't believe her. She was also pretty sure he wasn't going to let her go. She really wished she had called Peter. She looked down at Sampson and petted his head.

"Well, I apologize for intruding, and I'll keep him on his leash from here on out. We'll be leaving now. Once again, I'm truly sorry."

Daniel finally spoke, and when he did, Jess was terrified. "Jess, I know you're lying. Don't insult my intelligence."

Jess was speechless.

Daniel continued, "I see this going one of two ways. Option number one is that you can turn over your phone and walk away and forget everything you think you know, and I won't press charges, and your husband won't go through the humiliation of finding out his wife was illegally trespassing. I do have the power to destroy his reputation thanks to you. Option number two is that I call David and he will come with lights and sirens blaring, and I can make a formal charge and he can arrest you. It's your choice, Jess. Which option would you prefer?"

Jess tried to look just as ominous as Daniel. "You wouldn't do that. David will see your little illegal business and arrest you."

Daniel started to laugh. "Are you sure about that? You really don't know how small towns work, do you. Should we give that little hypothesis a try?" He pulled out his phone and looked at her.

Against her will, Jess found tears springing in her eyes. She angrily wiped them away. "Option one," she spat.

Daniel still looked livid. "Good. Well, then, hand over your phone."

"I don't have it."

"I don't believe you."

"I swear I'm not lying," Jess sobbed.

"Put your hands up and let me see."

Jess immediately put up her hands.

"Turn around and place your hands on the wall."

Jess panicked. "What are you going to do?"

He placed a hand on her breast. "I'm going to make sure that you're not lying." His hands slid down her side, then traveled to her buttocks.

Peter's voice rang out in the darkness. "Jess, where are you?"

Jess's eyes met Daniel's.

"You can go," Daniel said as he dropped his hands. He grabbed her arm as she turned to leave. "Not a word, do you understand? I promise you that if you say a word to anyone, I will make this look like we're having an affair. Then what will your precious husband think?"

Jess jerked her arm away and pulled Sampson along with her. She ran back towards her house.

"Peter," she said breathlessly when she entered their yard.

"Where have you been?" Peter demanded. "I was worried sick."

"I'm sorry. Sampson took off and ran into Daniel's yard. I was chasing him."

Peter narrowed his eyes. "You're lying. I can tell. He's on a leash, Jess, did he drag you along?"

Jess cleared her throat to contain her emotions. "No, he didn't drag me along. Some animal was in our yard, I think it was a raccoon. When Sampson spotted it, he ran after it, and I lost hold of his leash. We ended up over at Daniel's."

Peter grabbed her and hugged her. "I was worried sick when I couldn't find you." He released her and bent over to pet Sampson. "You did a good job protecting Jess, but next time, please contain it to our yard."

Jess blinked back tears, beyond grateful that Peter had called her name. Daniel was so close to finding her phone. She didn't know what she would have done if he'd found it.

They walked inside, and Peter led her back to bed.

"Peter, I don't think I'll be able to go back to sleep. I'm too wound up now."

Peter smiled. "Who said anything about sleep?"

"Well, in that case, I suppose I could go back to bed." She wrapped her arms around him and kissed him.

He scooped her up as he carried her to bed.

He gently laid her on the bed and pushed her hair back. They kissed softly at first then with more passion. His hand traveled up to her breast.

She gasped and tried to block out the image of Daniel frisking her, looking for her phone. Her phone. Still hidden inside her pants.

Jess squirmed under Peter and then rolled him over on his back. She kissed him, then pushed herself off of him. Slowly and carefully, she undressed as she made sure her phone remained in her pants as she stripped down. Climbing back into bed, she slowly started to unbutton Peter's shirt.

He stopped her. "Why are your hands shaking?" he asked with concern.

Instead of answering right away, she bent over and kissed him again. Then she whispered, "I want you." She needed to feel empowered and in control. She needed to be the one in charge, the one who initiated what would happen, the one who determined how it would end.

After they finished, Jess rolled off of him and they lay breathless on the bed.

"That was incredible," Peter said as he pulled her to him.

Jess cuddled up tight against him. She felt safe lying beside him listening to his breathing and she smiled to herself when she heard him drifting off to sleep.

Her thoughts went back to the shed. *What should I do,* she wondered. She wanted to turn Daniel in, but who could she go to? Originally, she had planned on going to David, but now she didn't trust him. Daniel was too close to David. She wasn't sure if David would truly investigate Daniel's illegal dealings, or if he'd tell Daniel what she had done. She didn't want to single-handedly ruin Peter's career. She needed to weigh her options. Maybe she could travel out of town and contact law enforcement farther in another town. The problem was, she didn't know how far Daniel's loyal minions extended.

Peter was gone when she woke the next morning. She reached for her phone and looked at the photos she had taken from the night before. She had him. She knew she did. All she had to do was get these pictures to the right people. Who that was, she wasn't sure.

Jess walked up into her office and fished around in her desk until she took out a flash drive. There wasn't going to be any chance of being caught with these pictures on her phone.

A notification popped up indicating that the pictures had transferred to the flash drive, so she erased them from her phone. Looking down at the flash drive in her hand, she wondered what to do next. She wasn't going to stay home alone, that was for sure.

Grabbing her running gear, Jess quickly got dressed, and grabbed Sampson's leash. She stepped outside and looked around to make sure Daniel wasn't waiting to pounce. With Sampson by her side, she led him to the edge of the road and began running in the opposite direction of Daniel's house.

About a quarter mile in, she heard a truck slow down behind her. She continued jogging, waiting for it to go around. It didn't. Looking behind her, she motioned for it to go past. Jess stumbled on a lose rock but caught herself and continued to run. She motioned for the truck to pass again and when the truck still didn't go around, she stopped and jogged in place waiting for it to go by. Her heart sped up when she saw the thug with the scar along the side of his face following behind her. She looked around and felt panicked when she saw that the only thing surrounding her were trees and a creek flowing rapidly a few feet from the road.

Her pace quickened and the truck sped up a little faster. "Sampson," she urged as she pulled the leash and quickly turned around to run back towards her house. The engine revved as the tired squealed and the truck did a U turn in the middle of the road. It quickly pulled up beside her. The power window rolled down. Out of breath, she stopped and turned to look at the driver.

He smiled menacingly at her with darkened teeth. Then he pulled out a pistol and pointed it at her head.

Jess screamed and fell to the ground. The sound of his laughter echoed in her ears as the truck sped away, leaving a rubber tire track in its wake.

When she could no longer hear the truck and she had stopped shaking, she stood up. Sampson was sniffing at her and nudged her with his nose. Angrily, she dusted herself off. “Some guard dog you’re going to be,” she muttered to Sampson.

She jogged back home with Sampson at her side. After hopping in the shower and then getting dressed, she grabbed her phone and tucked it in her back pocket. Before leaving the house, she grabbed Sampson’s leash, clicked it on his collar, and led him out to the car. Sampson hopped in the passenger side of the car and sat down on the seat. Jess shut the door and walked over to the driver’s side.

She thought for a minute, pulled out her phone. typed the words **police department** and clicked on the search icon. A box popped up, asking Jess if her phone had permission to know her location. She clicked yes and looked for the farthest police department that was still in her county. Once she had the directions that she wanted she started up her car.

The radio was blaring from the speakers as a distraction of what she was about to do. She checked her rear-view mirror and almost screamed. The same big black pickup truck with a chrome grill was right behind her. Gripping the steering wheel tightly and she drew in a deep breath. The truck was coming closer and closer. She sped up, and it sped up. She slowed down, and it slowed down.

Trying to remain calm, Jess scanned the area trying to find a driveway to pull into where someone could be a witness if he shot her. There was nothing around except trees, water, or boulders. Jess pushed the accelerator down to the floor. If she was going to die, then she was going to go her own way, and not by someone's bullet.

It wasn't long before she saw the truck pulling up along the driver's side. She waited for it to be right next to her, then slammed on her brakes. The truck continued down the road.

Shaking, Jess turned onto a side road and kept driving. She turned onto another side road and when she was sure that the truck was nowhere in sight she pulled off onto the shoulder. Not knowing what to do next she sat there shaking. Sampson was moving nervously back and forth in the car. Tears streamed down her face, and she was gasping for air. Her chest felt tight, and she was afraid she might be having a heart attack. She tried to slow her breathing, and the tears finally stopped flowing.

In hindsight, she wished she had gotten his license plate. Sampson whined and laid back down. When she stopped shaking, she pulled back onto the road. She kept looking in her rear-view mirror, waiting for the truck to come flying out of nowhere, but it didn't. After an hour of driving, she began to relax. She no longer had a destination in mind, but knew wherever it would be, it would be far away from Daniel.

Sampson started to whine, and Jess absently reached over to pet him. She pulled into the visitor's parking lot for Minekill Falls. Grabbing the leash, she led Sampson out of the car. She knew the pup needed to stretch, and, truth be told, so did she.

They hiked down to the falls. He walked over to lap up the fresh, cool water, and she sat on a log, watching the water cascade over the falls. The sound was soothing, and for the first time all day, she could stop and think.

She couldn't tell Peter. Even with the pictures, he would just tell her to mind her own business because it would ruin his business if she told. She couldn't tell David; he might believe her, but chances were, he'd warn Daniel, and Daniel would come after her.

Should she drive down to the city? But really, who could she trust? New York City was rampant with drugs, and for all she knew, Daniel was a supplier. She thought about Albany, but once again, it was a big city, and drugs were pervasive in all big cities. She didn't know how far Daniel's supply chain went, but she wasn't taking any chances.

"Sampson, come," Jess yelled. He turned from the water and came trotting up to her. She took his leash and began leading him back up the hill towards the car.

By the time they had reached the top, other people were starting to fill up the parking lot. A dad with a small, curly-haired girl sitting on his back, strapped tightly in a backpack, was pulling a hat off her head. The girl's mom, who seemed about Jess's age, exited the passenger side of the SUV. Jess wondered if she and Peter would ever have kids. After all of this was over, she wondered if their names would ever be synonymous again.

Sampson hopped into the car, and Jess continued to drive north until her phone finally had cell service. She pulled over and called Peter. He picked up after the third ring.

"Hi darling," she said trying to sound as nonchalant as possible. "I've decided to drive down to see my parents for the evening. I thought a surprise visit would be nice."

"Well, that's a surprise for me, too," he said. "Why don't you wait until the weekend, and I'll drive down with you?"

"No bother," Jess said. "I know you're busy with your clients and you mentioned having court on Monday. Now that I think of it, I might stay a night or two."

There was silence on the other end of the phone. Finally, Peter said, "Jess, is everything alright? This isn't like you to just up and leave for a few days without discussing it with me, first."

Jess blinked back tears. She cleared her throat and said, "Everything is fine, Peter, really. I just need some time away from the solitude. It's a big adjustment, and I just need to find my bearings. Please understand. I need to do this for myself."

Jess could hear the secretary's voice in the background. Peter mumbled something to his secretary. "I've got to go. I have a meeting with a client. Jess, I love you."

"I love you, too. I'll see you Monday night."

Jess clicked off the phone and looked over at Sampson. "Well, boy, looks like we're taking a road trip."

She reached for her sunglasses and continued driving north.

After about three hours, she pulled into a gas station in Lake George. While she was filling up her tank, her eyes scanned various buildings. She hadn't seen a police station yet and wasn't sure if she felt safe enough to do that. Next, she looked for the black truck and breathed a sigh of relief that there was no truck in sight. The pump kicked off, and she placed the nozzle back in the holder. She moved her car to a parking spot and pulled out her phone searching for a Private Investigator and was surprised to see there was one in the area. In the contact box, she typed her information and was pleased to see an automated message saying she would be getting a call soon.

Jess let out a sigh of relief. This was a much better plan than going to the police. Things were finally falling into place.

After backing out of the parking spot, she put the car in drive and headed west. She searched for nearby hotels that allowed pets, and found the Star Motel, two miles down the road. Sampson stayed in the car as she registered and paid for her room in cash. The last thing she wanted to do was make Peter think she was having an affair by having the charge turn up on a credit card statement. Jess began to relax as she sat down on the bed. She scanned the simple room with relief. She took a shower and tried to get the image of the man pointing a gun at her out of her head.

As she was getting dressed in the same clothes she'd had on before, the phone rang causing her to jump.

"Hello?" she asked anxiously.

"Hello, Mrs. Stanton. You were inquiring about my services?" a man's voice on the other end replied.

"Yes, I did. I'm afraid of discussing this over the phone, but I'm in trouble and I need your help. Can you help me?"

"Well, that depends," replied the man. "Can you meet me at a little diner on Broad Street in about an hour?"

"Sure," replied Jess. "Can you tell me the name and address? I'm not from the area."

"Kelly's Kitchen. 107 Broad Street. You can't miss it."

Jess wrote down the information and said, "I'll see you then."

Chapter 11

Jess arrived at the diner 20 minutes early. She was ravenous. The waitress came over and took her drink order. She looked at the menu and decided on a burger and fries. As she waited, she scrolled through her phone and then quickly stopped. It suddenly occurred to her that she didn't have a charger. The last thing she needed was for her phone to die while she was here. She fished around in her purse and felt the flash drive sitting at the bottom. She would feel better once she got the pictures into someone else's hands.

She looked around at the decor in the diner. Over the tops of the windows hung white valances with blue embroidered flowers. The tables and chairs were made of heavy dark wood. The white walls displayed many pictures of the area. There was an old-time jukebox in the corner with an old country song crooning from the speakers.

She heard the bell above the door ring and turned her head. An older man walked in. She looked down at her watch, noting that the private investigator should be arriving soon. As she continued to look around, she was surprised to see the older gentleman walking towards her. Jess tried to hide her surprise.

He took a seat across from her and said, "Hello Mrs. Stanton. Nice to meet you. My name is George Myers. We spoke on the phone."

Jess nodded, unsure of how to act with this stranger sitting across from her. How did she start? What if someone overheard? Did the other people around her know what he did for a living? She was suddenly nervous.

The waitress appeared with Jess's order, and she looked at George. "Hi George, what are you having today?"

George smiled at her. "I'll take the usual, Abby. Thanks."

Abby laughed and shook her head. "I should have known, George," and walked away.

"I see you come here often," Jess said.

George leaned back and nodded. "Every chance I get. The food here is delicious."

Once Abby delivered George's coffee, George said, "Alright, now what's this all about?"

Jess looked around at the half-filled diner.

George read her thoughts. "It's fine. No one knows what I do, and I plan on keeping it that way. Sometimes the best places to hide are in the open."

"I think that's the motto my neighbor, Daniel, lives by. Which is actually why I am coming to you." Jess went on to tell George about how the former homeowners just disappeared, the note in the drawer, and how they had acquired the house at way below cost. Then she went on to tell him about the seemingly unending box truck deliveries, the warning that David had given her, and then nervously about what happened at the barn. She stopped talking when Abby delivered a hearty plate of pancakes, eggs over easy, bacon, sausage, and toast.

Jess momentarily forgot about her story. "You can't possibly eat all of that, can you?"

George smiled. "Every morsel. My doctors aren't happy about it, but you can't please everybody. Please go on."

Jess took a sip of her coffee, then continued telling him about Daniel's goons shooting targets and pointing a gun at her, and about the truck following her when she left the house that morning. She placed her purse on the table and fished around until she found what she was looking for. In her hand she held a flash drive and handed it to George. "I have proof, it's all on here."

George looked at it for a moment, and then pulled a USB adapter from his pocket. He connected the flash drive to his phone and started scrolling through the pictures. When he was finished, he asked, "How many deliveries a day did you say he usually gets?"

She pulled out her notebook, which she had tucked in her purse before she left that morning.

"It's all in here," she said. "At least three trucks pull in daily."

"And you said they all do business at that barn?"

"Yes."

"Can I keep the flash drive? I have someone who could check this out for me, and the pictures would really help him out."

"Sure," replied Jess with relief. She was so grateful that he believed her, and she was happy to not to be carrying around the burden of proof anymore.

He took another bite of toast and swallowed. "I would also suggest you destroy your phone. Buy a burner until this is all over."

"You're not going to contact David, are you?"

George shook his head. "No, in small towns like yours, it's hard to separate small town politics from the law. The guy I'm thinking of is trustworthy. I would trust him with my life, and believe me, I don't say that lightly. There are very few people that I trust."

For the first time in a long time, Jess felt like she was doing the right thing.

They ate in silence until George finally stopped and took a sip of his coffee. "I'll need you to write down his address and any employees that he has working for him. If you could provide a description, that would be even better."

Jess took out a pen and started writing. She spoke as she wrote. "I've only seen two men working for him. One has a scar across his cheek, and the other one is shorter and stocky. They are definitely not the friendly type."

George nodded. "Make sure you include that description. That would be helpful." He reached across the table and stopped her hand from writing.. "Jess, the fewer people who are near the house when my buddy checks this out, the better. I'd recommend that you stay here for a few days. I don't want him coming after you if this checks out."

. "My husband doesn't know that I'm here. In fact, he doesn't know anything about this. I told him I was visiting my parents and wouldn't be home until Monday. It'll look suspicious if I disappear for longer than a couple of days."

George studied her intently. "Look, Jess. It's up to you whether you go back or not, but in my professional opinion, I'm telling you not to. I'm assuming if your husband doesn't know about the pictures, then he doesn't know that you've contacted me?"

Jess shook her head no. "He's a lawyer. He just opened his new practice, and I didn't want to drag him into this. I've tried telling him my suspicions, but he doesn't believe me, so I left it at that. I don't want him connected with any fallout this might bring. It would ruin him."

"I see," George replied. "Jess, are you sure you want to do this? Once this thing is blown wide open, there's no going back."

Jess could feel her anger rising. "He's an illegal drug dealer, and you want me to just ignore it? You're kidding right?"

George took off his glasses and put them on the table. "No, ma'am. I'm not kidding. The reality is, once you start going after him, there will be repercussions. He will retaliate. Do you honestly think for a minute he's not going to suspect that you are behind this? There's lots of bad people in this world, Jess, who do lots of real bad things."

Jess could feel herself shaking. She didn't know if it was from rage or fear. "He's already started," she whispered.

George took a sip of coffee. "Started what?"

"Retaliation," she replied. "I'm fairly certain I'm being followed. I've had a gun pointed at me. No matter where I'm at or what I'm doing, I see one of his goons." She looked at George pleadingly. "I don't know what else to do."

George looked around the diner. "I know everyone in here, so no one has followed you into the diner, but they might be tracking your car. Do you think they know where you are?"

Jess shook her head. "No, I told my husband I was going to see my parents in the city. I haven't seen the truck that had been following me and I haven't seen anyone familiar since I've arrived in town."

George held out his hand. "Can I see your phone?"

He inspected her phone, looking for any tracking devices, but everything was clear. He handed it back to her and pushed his plate to the side. "Look, I don't mean to scare you, but if they are following you, then they most likely know, or at least suspect, that you have the pictures, and they know where you are. I'll give my friend a call and set this into motion, but unless you want to wind up dead, I suggest you stay out of sight. Stay away from anyone you know, and don't go anywhere. Do you understand?"

Jess nodded. Her throat went dry, and she suddenly felt nauseous. She sensed that her whole world had just flipped upside down.

George continued, "Get a burner phone and destroy this one. I've got the flash drive. Is there anything else incriminating that you have on you?"

"No," she answered.

"Good, then call your husband and tell him you're staying with your parents for a couple days longer. If you have to, get into an argument with him. Do what you have to, so that he's not suspicious. Do you understand?"

Jess's head reeled from all his directions. "I understand. I'll call him soon, and I'll stay in my room at the hotel. How long do you think that I have to stay out of sight?"

George shook his head. "Four days. Five days, tops."

"When will I know that it's over?"

"Honey, it's all just beginning. The sting itself will be over in a day or two. If I were you and your husband, I'd leave town and go far, far away. Men like Daniel don't mess around. He'll be angry, and he'll be looking for you."

This was more than Jess could process. She felt like the wind had just been knocked out of her, and she couldn't breathe. Her hands started to shake at the enormity of what George was saying. She pushed her plate away, no longer hungry.

She instantly regretted sneaking over to the barn. She should have minded her own business, like Peter had warned her to do. If she had, then none of this would be happening. Maybe they'd put Daniel behind bars for a long time. George was right. She couldn't go home, but with any luck, she'd get her life back. Peter would be mad and might leave her, but she refused to live in fear any longer.

"I'll stay here. I'll call and tell him I'm going to stay at my parents for a few more nights."

George took out his phone and made a call. "Henry, set up some extra patrols past the Star Motel down on Main. Thanks."

He shrugged and said, "Just as an extra precaution."

Jess looked at him apprehensively. "I never told you that I was staying at the Star Motel. How did you know that?"

George lifted an eyebrow. "I'm very good at what I do."

Jess wouldn't admit it, but she was relieved to have an extra pair of eyes watching out for her.

It was later in the afternoon when they were finally finished, and George went to the counter to pay the bill. They walked out of the diner together.

George stopped Jess before they reached their cars. "When it's safe for you to go back, I'll let you know. Until then, stay inside your room at the hotel."

They both climbed into their vehicles, George turning right as Jess turned left.

Jess's mind was still racing from everything that George had told her. She thought about Jason and his motorcycle accident. He was lucky to have survived it. All the surgeries, then the rehab. He was in so much pain all the time. The doctor prescribed pain medication. That helped some, but not completely. Then, when the pain meds stopped, he turned to other drugs trying to relieve the pain. Eventually, heroine became his drug of choice.

She had tried to help him. Hell, her whole family tried to help him, but you couldn't help someone who didn't want to be helped. When she thought of the day she lost her brother, it wasn't the day he died, it was the day of his motorcycle accident. Jess wiped away a tear. She thought of Daniel and his egotistical arrogance to expect to do whatever he wanted and just get away with it. Well, not this time. She was doing this for Jason, and everyone else who never had a chance. She would see Daniel behind bars if it was the last thing she did.

She stopped by a mom-and-pop shop and bought a burner phone. This didn't feel like her life anymore, but rather a horror movie. She paid for the phone in cash and walked out the door.

Sampson was lying on the bed waiting for her when she walked through the door. She lay down beside him and petted him. He had this way of calming her, and she began to feel better. She looked at the time. Peter would be getting home soon. She dialed the number and waited.

"Hey, Jess. How's your parents?"

She hated lying to him. "Dad's not the greatest. He's not feeling well. I thought maybe I would stay with them for a couple more days, just to make sure he's going to be alright."

"Is it serious?"

She could hear the concern in Peter's voice and hated herself for doing this to him.

"I don't think so, but at his age, you know how things can escalate," she replied.

"I know," Peter said. "I miss you."

Jess could feel tears start to burn her eyes. She blinked them away. "I miss you, too."

He must have heard her voice change. He had always been good at reading people. That's what made him a great lawyer. "Jess, are you alright?"

She nodded, even though he couldn't see her. She cleared her throat. "I'm fine. Really, I am." It remained quiet before she said, "Mom has dinner ready, so I really should go. I love you, and I'll talk to you tomorrow."

She hung up the phone, feeling more alone than she ever had. She hated lying to Peter. Hated staying here alone in a hotel, hundreds of miles from home. She hated Daniel for putting her through this, and she couldn't wait to get him behind bars where he belonged. She looked at her phone one last time before she destroyed it. It was like cutting the lifeline to those she cared about. Now she was truly alone.

Sampson whined and needed to go out. Jess grabbed his leash and walked him outside. She tried to stay close to her room in case she needed to duck inside quickly. As Sampson sniffed his surroundings, she scanned the area looking for the truck that was following her earlier. She was relieved to see that it was nowhere to be found. Someone with dark clothes was walking through the parking lot. They were too far for her to see if it was one of Daniel's goons. She prayed it wasn't. Jess and Sampson went back inside and settled in for the night. She had a feeling it was going to be a very long night.

Chapter 12

It was two in the morning. The DEA were lined up, guns drawn as they descended upon Daniel's house with the sole purpose of putting Daniel away. They wore respirators to protect them from chemicals in the event they discovered a meth lab. The house was dark, and nothing was moving inside. Some of the agents split up and went to the shed. They motioned to one another so that the sting operation would happen at the same time in both places.

The signal was given, and battering rams slammed against the front doors of both places. DEA agents began running through the house, yelling, guns drawn.

Victoria jumped from the bed and screamed. She grabbed her clothes and quickly began to get dressed. She looked beside her and became more terrified to see that Daniel wasn't lying there beside her.

Daniel was lying on the floor in the barn with his hands behind his back and handcuffs around his wrists. He was yelling at them. "I'll have your badges for this!"

An agent knelt down beside him and said, "For what?"

Daniel didn't say another word as the agents took pictures of bowls, scales, measuring cups, and bags of meth. They also confiscated bricks of marijuana. Daniel seethed as he watched everything that he had worked for being bagged, tagged, and taken away. He would get even.

The first thing he would do was contact David and see what the hell this was all about. They had an understanding, and David knew if he minded his own business, he could count on Daniel when he needed something. Not anymore.

He looked around. None of these guys looked familiar to him. Something more must be going on. These guys were the big time. Not the local police, but the freaking DEA. The thought of Jess popped into his mind. She had something to do with it. He could feel it. He should have had her taken care of when she started snooping around, but he knew it would draw too much attention. He didn't know how much her husband knew, but he would find out, and there would be hell to pay.

In the background, he could hear Victoria yelling, "Get your hands off me! Daniel! Daniel!" He could hear the cop rattling off the Miranda rights. He turned his head and saw her being put into the back of a car.

He was hoisted to his feet by a big, burly agent. Daniel kept silent as they read him his rights and led him to a different car.

Two hours later, after fingerprints and mugshots, he sat seething, alone in the interrogation room. He had requested a lawyer and was refusing to say another word until one arrived. He would get even with everyone who had a part in this. He would make sure of that.

Peter walked in with his briefcase. He sat across from Daniel.

"Hi Daniel, I was told you requested me as your lawyer."

Daniel looked up at him and replied, "I did."

"I should advise you that since we're neighbors, I'm probably not the best choice for you, and I have not represented anyone in a case of this importance. I normally represent people with misdemeanors or a client who is charged with a DUI. I can refer you to someone with more experience in these matters who will do a great job for you."

Daniel shook his head. "I chose you, and you will make all of this go away."

Peter stood up and shut his briefcase. "I don't appreciate your tone, and I don't have to represent you. Like I said before. I will give you some names of people who you can hire."

Daniel's patience was gone. "Sit down, Peter. I'm not finished."

Peter stood up. "I believe we are."

Peter was walking towards the door when Daniel said, "Do you know where your wife is right now?"

Peter turned around. "What are you talking about?"

Daniel knew he had his attention. "If you don't want your precious little wife to have a mishap, perhaps you should reconsider. The things that could happen to her could be quite nasty."

Peter sat back down. "You can't threaten me or my family. I can make sure you're behind bars for a long time."

Daniel smiled. "No, you can't, and I'm not bluffing. Where is your wife right now? She's not at home."

"Not that it's any of your business, but she's with family."

Daniel shook his head with pity. "Oh, Peter, she's lying to you." He looked at Peter and could see the confusion on his face. He egged him on. "Go ahead, call her. See if she's where she says she is."

He looked at Daniel and said, "I'm going to leave. Good luck in finding a lawyer."

****

Peter picked up his briefcase and walked out. The minute he reached his car, he called Jess's parents. Her father answered the phone.

"Hello, Walt," Peter said. "How are you feeling?"

Walt sounded surprised at hearing his son-in-law's voice. "I'm fine, Peter. Is everything alright? It's awfully early for a phone call."

Peter looked at his watch and groaned. It was only five in the morning. "I'm sorry, Walt. I wasn't paying attention to the time. Jess said you weren't feeling well. I'm glad to hear you're alright. Is she around? I'd like to speak with her."

Walt's tone turned serious. "She's not here, Peter. In fact, we haven't seen her since the last time you two came for a visit. Is everything alright?"

Peter cleared his throat, "Yes, Walt, everything's alright. She had mentioned wanting to visit, but now that I think about it, she said she couldn't because she had a work conference to go to. Sorry for the confusion."

Peter hung up and got out of his car. He walked back inside the precinct and asked to speak with Daniel again. He waited until Daniel was escorted back to see him.

Daniel sat at the table, looking smug.

"Where is she, you son of a bitch?! What have you done with her?" he demanded.

Daniel grinned condescendingly. "Peter, this isn't the movies. You act like she's being tortured or something. She's perfectly safe. For now, that is. You can check for yourself. She's at the Star Motel in Lake George, room number three."

Peter took out his phone and looked up the number for the Star Motel.

"Star Motel, how can I help you?"

Peter looked at Daniel as he spoke. "Please connect me to room number 3."

The receptionist did so. The phone rang and rang and rang. There was no answer.

Now it was Peter's turn to look smug. "It appears you were wrong, Daniel."

Daniel spat, "You stupid fool. She knows better than to answer the hotel phone when she thinks no one knows where she is. Call her cell."

Peter dialed her cell phone, but there was no answer. He dialed again but had no success. He looked at Daniel and said, "Let's assume that I do take on your case. What will happen to my wife?"

Daniel shrugged. "Nothing, as long as you clear me of the charges."

Peter studied Daniel, then stood up, picking up his briefcase. "I'll think about it."

"Don't think too long," Daniel warned.

Peter went out to the car and tried Jess's phone again. Again, no answer. He looked up the number for the Star Motel. He dialed. The receptionist answered.

"Can you connect me to room 3?" Peter requested.

It wasn't long before the phone rang. He listened, hoping Jess would pick up. She didn't.

He called the receptionist again.

"Can you please check and see if Jess Stanton is in her room? She's not answering the phone, but it's a family emergency, and I'm trying to reach her."

"Yes, sir. Please hold."

Ten minutes later, Peter heard Jess's voice.

"Peter? Is everything alright? How did you know I was here?"

"Daniel told me," Peter replied. "How ironic that he would know where my wife is, and I don't. Jess, what's going on?"

"I can't tell you, Peter. It's for your own protection, I swear. Just know that I'm safe, and I'll tell you everything when I get home."

Peter laughed bitterly. "My wife and her flair for the dramatic. You know what, don't tell me what's going on. I could probably ask Daniel and he'd tell me. Jesus, Jess, what the hell did you get mixed up in? I told you to mind your own business."

Jess was quiet on the other end of the phone then she whispered, "What should I do?"

"I don't know, but we'll talk later. Right now, I have to speak with Daniel."

"Peter don't!" she exclaimed. "He's dangerous."

"I know," he replied. "I really need to go."

He abruptly hung up and banged his hands on the steering wheel in frustration.

If she had only minded her own business, none of this would be happening right now. He climbed back out of the car and walked back into the jail. Once again, he requested to see Daniel.

Peter was pacing the room when Daniel entered, smiling.

Peter glared at Daniel. "What do you want?"

Daniel leaned back in his chair, looking like he had just won a game of chess. "It's easy, all I want is for you to represent me and clear my name. That's what lawyers do, isn't it?"

"What about Jess?" Peter asked.

"What about her?" Daniel asked in return.

Peter was getting impatient. "Are you going to harm her?"

Daniel looked Peter in the eye. "I guess that depends on you, doesn't it? You do your job. Clear my name. We can forget this little inconvenience even happened. You keep your nosy wife in check, and perhaps I can forgive her transgression this time."

Peter hated the condescending tone that Daniel was using. He shrugged and said, "Your threats are empty. There's not much you can do from behind bars, Daniel. From where I'm sitting, I have all the power."

Daniel shrugged and shook his head. "You're a fool, Peter. I'm the one who holds the power in this town. Haven't you realized that yet? Hell, even your wife has figured that one out. I have associates that will make sure that things go as planned, and if you lose this case, your little law business, the one I helped you acquire, will probably go under. I mean, a lawyer who can't take care of one of the town's own. What kind of lawyer can you be?"

They stared at each other in silence, calculating what the next move would be.

Peter spoke first. "I'll do it. I'll represent you." He was seething.

"Good, I'm glad we've reached an understanding. Now get me out on bail, would you? I'm tired of looking at these drab walls."

Peter looked at his watch. "It's Saturday morning, you won't be arraigned until Monday."

Daniel leaned back in his chair and calmly studied Peter. He put his hands together with his fingertips touching. The silence that rested between them was suffocating. Finally, Daniel spoke.

"Sorry, Peter, that just won't do. I need to be released today. Your wife has caused enough damage, and although I am a patient man, my patience is wearing thin."

Peter tried not to let his fear show on his face. "It's a weekend. There's nothing I can do."

Daniel leaned forward. "There's always something you can do." He slammed his hand on the table. "Figure it out!"

Daniel stood up to leave. He banged on the door until the guard opened it. "We're done here," he growled.

Peter shut his briefcase and stood to leave. He tried to keep his expression neutral when the guard looked at him. He tried to act as though this nightmare wasn't happening. He wished he could go back in time. He pulled out his phone and started to dial Jess's number. Then he stopped and hung up. Why had she lied to him? He couldn't process this now. There was no time.

He looked at his contacts and pressed on the name Harold Duthmore.

A man's voice answered on the other line.

"Hi, Judge Duthmore, this is Peter Stanton. I'm sorry for calling so early, but I was hoping to ask a favor."

"How are you, Peter? What's going on?"

"Well sir, to be honest, I need a big favor. I have a client who is being held for an arraignment on Monday. I'd like for him to be released now on his own recognizance and appear in court on Monday."

The judge's tone turned serious. "This is a mighty big favor, and highly unusual. Who is the client?"

"Daniel Easton, sir."

There was silence on the other end.

"Hello?" Peter asked, after what seemed a few seconds had gone by.

"WHO IN THE HELL WOULD ARREST DANIEL EASTON!" Judge Duthmore bellowed.

Peter cleared his throat. Although he was fairly certain his wife had something to do with this, he wasn't about to say so. He looked up at the ceiling. "According to the DEA, it was an anonymous tip in another county, sir."

Judge Duthmore retorted back, "It won't be anonymous for long. Daniel has a way of finding things out. God help the poor bastard that started this shit storm."

Peter felt sweat trickle down his back. "Sir, is it possible to set my client free until Monday morning?"

Judge Duthmore didn't hesitate. "Yes, I'll call the station now. Your client is free to go and will report to court first thing Monday morning."

"Thank you, sir."

Judge Duthmore spoke again. "Peter, you haven't been in town long enough to really get to know Daniel Easton. Let me give you a piece of advice. If you're smart, you'll try and find a way to get out of Daniel's case. Maybe disappear for a while, if you know what I mean. It's not going to end well for you or your wife if you lose."

Peter was quiet for a moment, then replied, "Thank you, sir. I appreciate the advice, but I have no intention of losing."

He hung up the phone and let out a sigh of relief. He walked down to the little diner around the corner. He'd have a cup of coffee and think all of this through before going back into the jail. Plus, it wouldn't hurt for Daniel to sit and stew for a while. The pompous, arrogant ass.

An hour later, he walked back to the precinct and once again requested Daniel. He waited patiently in the interview room until he was brought in. He smiled inwardly at the shackles that bound Daniel like the common criminal that he was. Daniel walked over and sat down across from him.

"You're free to go," Peter said in an even tone.

Daniel smiled at him. "I knew you'd find a way."

Peter stood and slipped on his jacket as he continued, "You will need to be at the courthouse on Monday at 8 a.m. for the arraignment. As your lawyer, I'm asking you to be there half an hour early."

Daniel started to walk towards the door. "I'll be there. You just better be prepared to keep me out of jail."

With that, he shut the door behind him, and Peter sat back down at the table, trying to think of a way out of this.

Peter warily stood up and walked through the offices and then outside. He was mentally exhausted, and physically sick to his stomach. His phone rang. He didn't recognize the phone number but listened to the voicemail.

"Peter, it's Jess. I just bought a burner phone. If you want to talk, call me at this number. I'm sorry. I love you."

A burner phone? An irate judge? Daniel knowing where Jess was when he didn't? What had Jess gotten him into?

****

Jess dialed George. The phone rang twice before she heard his voice.

"Hello?"

"George? It's Jess. I'm in trouble."

"What's happened?"

"I talked to Peter, and they know where I am. They told Peter where I was. They even knew my room number. George, what do I do?

"I warned you that they would retaliate. I'm just surprised they found you so quickly. Did you get rid of your phone?"

"Yes, and I've stayed inside and haven't gone anywhere."

"Did you tell Peter why you were here?"

"No, I told him he was better off not knowing. He wasn't happy with me, but he didn't push it."

"Let me call my contact with the force and see what's going on."

They hung up. Jess paced the floor, wondering what to do next. Sampson stood up and looked around. It wasn't long before the phone rang again.

"Jess, I think it would be for the best if you moved to another hotel. I already have you registered under an assumed name. I'll have an officer pick you up in half an hour. Will that be long enough to gather your belongings?"

Jess looked around at the empty room. She didn't really have anything, because she didn't come here thinking she was going to stay. "That's plenty of time," she replied. "I'll be ready."

"Good. Look, when the officer comes to pick you up, make sure you see his badge. It's just a precaution. Don't call anyone to tell them you're switching hotels. Not even Peter. Just lay low. Do you understand?"

"I understand," Jess replied. "What about my car?"

"Your car?" George asked.

"Yes, it's in the parking lot."

"I'll have my buddy on the force tow it to the precinct. They'll check it over to make sure it's safe and there's no trackers attached to it, then they'll drop it off at the hotel."

"Thank you, George. I don't know what I would do without you."

****

Half an hour later, there was a knock on the door. Jess looked out the peephole in the door and saw an officer standing in front of the door. She cracked the door open. She felt silly but trusted George, so she said, "Can I see your badge?"

The officer quickly produced his badge, and Jess opened the door wider. Sampson was sitting at her feet. The officer stood in the doorway while she collected her few things, and they walked to the police car in silence. As they drove away, she looked at the shops, hotels, and gas stations whizzing past. They were on the outskirts of town by the time they finally stopped.

The officer got out of the car and opened the door for Jess. He produced a hotel key card and said, "You're already registered under the name of Kate Smyth. For your own safety, don't leave the room or call anyone. We're shorthanded tonight, but we'll try and patrol this area more frequently. Is there anything you need?"

Jess shook her head no. She walked with the officer as he led her into the room and left. The room was nicer than the one she was in previously. It had a king-sized bed, and a small refrigerator already filled with water and snacks. The carpet under her feet was soft, and the pillows on the bed were already beckoning to her.

She slipped off her shoes and crawled onto the bed. Sampson hopped up beside her. They both lay there in silence, and for the first time in a while, Jess finally felt safe.

Chapter 13

Daniel stormed into the Sheriff's office. "David, what the hell is going on?"

David leaned back in his chair and looked up at Daniel, shaking his head. "I wish I knew. I've been trying to find out ever since I found out you were arrested. This didn't come from me, and if I knew about it, I would have shut it down."

Daniel glared at him with disgust and sat down in the old leather chair across from him. "Make this go away."

David shrugged and sighed. "I've been trying, but they're keeping things tight-lipped. The only information I have is that the informant was anonymous."

Daniel leaned forward and asked, "Who are 'they'?"

"The DEA."

"Damn it! If I go down, then I'm taking you and this whole town with me." He glared at David and shouted, "I'm starting with you!"

Daniel banged a fist on David's desk and stood up. He leaned over the desk and said menacingly, "I'm telling you, David. Make.

This. Go. Away." He left without another word, slamming the door after him.

David opened his desk drawer and pulled out his flask of whiskey. It usually calmed his nerves, but not today. The last thing he needed was to be on Daniel Easton's bad side. He muttered under his breath as he picked up his phone and dialed the Attorney General's office. Once he was put through to the Attorney General, he wasted no time with small talk.

"Audrey, it's David. It appears you had a big bust go down in my part of the state. Care to tell me why I wasn't included?"

"It's nothing personal, David. We had a lead on the case, and time was of the essence. Surely, you can understand that. We wanted to grab Easton quietly without a lot of hoopla. You know how powerful people can manipulate the system."

"What do you mean by 'manipulate the system'? Are you insinuating that I'm in Daniel's pocket?"

There was silence on the other end of the phone. "Look, should we have notified you as a courtesy? Yes. Am I going to explain why we didn't? No. I'm very busy, as I'm sure you are, too. Good day, David." She hung up the phone.

"Damn it!" David muttered as he slammed down the phone. He thought about driving to her office and giving her a piece of his mind. The Attorney General wasn't telling him anything he couldn't read in the newspapers. He hoped like hell that they didn't suspect him of working with Daniel, but why else wouldn't they include him in the bust? It didn't make sense. He'd have to make sure all of his tracks were covered. The last thing he needed was the feds snooping around in his town.

David grabbed his hat and his keys, stormed outside, and got into his car. *Dammit,* he thought. He needed to get the answers that Daniel wanted. This nightmare had to disappear and fast. The first thing he needed to do was find out who the informant was. That should put him back in Daniel's good graces.

He put the cruiser into drive and drove towards Peter's office. He walked up to the door and saw that his office was closed. David banged on the door and looked through the window to make sure that he wasn't there. The office was dark. Peter's secretary wasn't even working which surprised him because he had assumed Peter would be working on Daniel's case. Maybe not. Maybe he didn't have enough experience and Daniel had hired someone else. Either way, Peter should be able to get the information that David needed to handle this matter.

He turned his car around and drove towards Peter's house. When he drove past Daniel's house, David was relieved to see that Daniel wasn't outside. He didn't want to succumb to

Daniel's wrath a second time. Peter's truck was parked in the driveway and David breathed a sigh of relief. *Now for some answers,* he mumbled as he stepped out of his cruiser and climbed the three steps leading to the porch. With the ring of the doorbell, he waited impatiently for Peter to answer.

When the door opened, David was surprised at how disheveled he looked. His hair was sticking up every which way. He looked like he had slept in his clothes, and he needed a shave.

Peter looked quizzically at David. "Can I help you, David?"

"Are you alright?" David asked. "You look like death warmed over."

Peter ran a hand through his hair. "I'm fine. Just working on a tough case. Thought I could use the peace and quiet, so I decided to work from home today."

David had a suspicion about the tough case that Peter was working on, but he didn't say anything.

David took off his hat. "I'm hoping you can help me out with something. Can I come in?"

Peter stepped back, and David walked through the door. The men walked into the kitchen and sat down across from each other.

"I had a visit from Daniel," said David. "He isn't real happy about how things are going."

Peter looked at him in surprise. "You had a visit from Daniel? He was just released not too long ago. What do you know?"

David took a long breath. He was out of patience. "What I know is that a member of my community was arrested. That there were DEA agents storming his house. This was a big bust. Lots of people were involved, but I, the sheriff, had no knowledge that this was going on in my own town. Lastly, I know there's a very pissed off, powerful man who wants some answers."

David continued to study Peter's face as he was telling him this, looking to see if Peter would reveal anything.

Peter's face remained stoic as he looked at David. "What exactly do you want from me?"

"I want to know what is going on with this case."

Peter ran a hand through his hair. "Daniel is my client, and whatever I know is lawyer-client privilege. I can't tell you what is going on, but you already know that."

David was getting more frustrated. "Who was the informant?"

Peter looked at him incredulously. "You can't ask me that. It was anonymous, but once again, you already know that. I don't know who the informant is, and really, that is the least of Daniel's problems."

David stood up and began pacing in the kitchen. He stopped and sat back down. This wasn't going well. He wasn't getting much from Peter, but he wasn't known for giving up easily. "Look, Peter, we're working for the same team, here. What can I do to help?"

Peter took a sip of coffee and calmly set down his cup. "What did Daniel tell you about the case?"

David had no choice other than to lie. Daniel hadn't told him anything about the case, except to make it go away. "The DEA confiscated drugs at his house."

Peter waited. "And?"

David took a stab in the dark. "And he wants to know who it was that tipped them off."

Peter looked at him skeptically. "And what else did he specifically tell you about the case?"

David felt like he was being backed into a corner. First the District Attorney insinuated that he was a dirty cop, and now Peter was playing cat and mouse. There were too many people becoming involved, and he didn't like it. His hands tightened into fists.

"Look, he wants me to clean up this mess," David spat. "Do you know where the evidence is stored?"

Peter sarcastically snapped, "What are you going to do? Destroy the evidence?" One look at David's face said it all. "Never mind," Peter retorted, "I don't want to know. Look, right now, he's out of jail until the trial. We still have time. Let's just both work it from our respective ends and see where we land. We'll get him out of it one way or the other. We don't have a choice, do we?"

David stood and stretched. "I'm going to take a drive up to Voorheesville and poke around there. The Attorney General is involved, so I'm sure the feds are storing the evidence there. I'll see where they are with the case and who the informant is. I'm sure they know, since that person might be called to trial. I'll see what I can find out."

Peter nodded. "David, can I ask you something?"

"Sure."

"Why do you want to find out who the informant is? Shouldn't you be more worried about the evidence?"

"There's a lot you can tell about an informant. If they are credible or not. I mean, if someone was accusing you of dealing drugs, wouldn't you like to know who it is? Plus, the informant is going to have to take the stand anyway."

Peter studied David. "Aren't you putting the informant in danger by releasing their name? I mean, there's a reason they want to remain anonymous."

David picked up his hat and put it on his head. "That's not my problem. Daniel wants to know who it was."

Peter stood up and started pacing. He shook his head. "It would make things worse for Daniel if anything were to happen to the informant. Trust me, David, if you want to help Daniel, stop looking for the informant, and instead try to find a mistake the DEA made so I can get him off on a technicality."

David shrugged, "I can try, but I can't make any promises. Daniel wants answers."

Peter cleared his throat. "I'll talk to Daniel and see what he wants to do. Maybe it would be best for the three of us sit down and make a plan."

****

David pulled up in front of the Albany County precinct in Voorheesville. He walked up to the counter and showed his badge. "I need to talk to the sheriff," he said, wasting no time on pretense.

The person at the counter picked up a phone and dialed some numbers. When he hung up, he said, "You can walk through those doors and his office is on the left."

David turned and walked through the doors. He gave a courtesy knock when he reached the sheriff's door and stepped inside.

"Sheriff Raycliff, I'm David Sutton. May I speak to you?"

"Sure, come on in."

“Thank you, sir. I’m sure you are aware of the drug bust the DEA just carried out in my town.”

The sheriff smiled. “I am. It was a hell of a bust. What seems to be the problem?”

David could still feel the indignation of being dismissed by the Attorney General. “Well, sir, that bust happened in my town. I didn’t even know it was going down. I was hoping I could be included in the investigation?”

Sheriff Raycliff smiled. “Well, that’s generous of you, David. We’d appreciate that.”

David continued talking. “I’d like to see the file on the case and fill in some holes if I can. I heard the informant was anonymous. If I can see who it was, I could also let you know about their credibility.”

He stood up. “Thanks for coming in, David. If we have any questions, we’ll be sure to reach out. We had strict orders from the top to keep the informant anonymous. I’m sure you understand. My hands are tied.”

David couldn’t believe what he was hearing. What happened to professional courtesy between precincts? He stood and shook hands with Sheriff Raycliff. “I understand. Thanks for seeing me.” He started leave, then stopped at the doorway and turned around. “By the way, I hope that informant of yours won’t have to stand trial.”

“Why is that?” Sheriff Raycliff asked.

"Because they'll never see the inside of a courthouse."

"Is this a threat, David?"

"No, sir. It's a fact. I know how information is leaked to the media, and without knowing who the informant is, my hands are tied. If you don't think he won't find out, then you're wrong."

David turned to leave. Once he was in his car, he threw his hat on the passenger seat in frustration. His only hope was to reach out to his contact at the news station and see if he could find out who the informant was. Somehow, his contact always managed to get the inside story. Why was everyone stonewalling him? Did they know he was working for Daniel? He suspected they did-- why else would everyone act dismissively? He had to figure a way out of this mess.

He put his car in gear and pulled out of the parking lot. As he drove west, he started thinking about the day Jess came into his office complaining about Daniel and suspecting him of drug trafficking. He had played dumb when she brought it up, but he knew she suspected something. Could she have been the informant? She would have known the comings and goings at Daniel's house. She would have had to have proof. The DEA wouldn't have gotten involved without it.

Who else could it have been? Should he tell Daniel? What proof did he have, except her visit to him months ago? Would Daniel blame him when he found out that David kept this from him? Probably. Maybe this never would have happened if David had just told Daniel in the beginning. No, he couldn't tell Daniel his suspicions now. It would be suicide. He'd have to find out some other way. There was always another way.

Chapter 14

Jess woke up to the blaring sound of her phone. She reached over and looked at the time. It was two in the morning. Who would be calling her at two in the morning? Her first thought was Daniel. She was afraid to answer it, but then she thought of Peter. It had been two days since they had argued. She answered it.

"Hello?" she asked hesitantly.

"Jess?" Peter replied.

She felt a rush of relief. "Is everything alright?"

Peter replied sadly, "I guess that would depend on your definition of alright."

"Peter, I'm so sorry. I'll tell you everything, I swear. I'm not cheating, but I had no other choice."

Peter cut her off. "Don't."

"Peter, please, just hear me out. I need you to listen to me."

"Don't," he repeated.

Before Jess could say another word, Peter continued, "I'm representing Daniel in court. I don't want to hear the truth. I don't want to hear your speculation. I can't."

Jess froze. When she found her voice, she gripped her phone tightly. "You can't be defending that sorry excuse for a human. You just can't. Did you forget that my brother died of an overdose? Please tell me you're better than that."

"Maybe if you'd been honest and up-front from the beginning, things could have been different. Maybe if you had minded your own business like I said from the beginning, things could have been different. Maybe if you had an ounce of common sense and stayed out of other people's lives, things could have been different. Now it's too late. You've created a storm that's going to have serious repercussions."

Jess couldn't believe what she was hearing. "Are you serious right now? You are blaming me for Daniel being arrested. He is a criminal. He--" Jess stopped as she heard the click of the phone. He had hung up on her.

She called back. It went immediately to voicemail. "Peter, you've got to listen to me. I have proof. Real proof that can put Daniel away. You don't have to defend him. Call me and I can explain everything." Jess hung up the phone. She was antsy and didn't want to leave things like this.

Sampson whined and nudged Jess's hand. "Hey boy, it's going to be alright. We'll work it out."

Jess couldn't give up. They needed to work this out. She called their home phone; it rang twice, then Peter hung up on her before she said a word. She called back and there was a busy signal. He had disconnected the phone.

She sat down, and Sampson whined again, signaling that he wanted to go outside. Wearily, she picked up his leash and clicked it on his collar. There was a light outside next to her door. She felt safer knowing she could see her surroundings. She led Sampson out to the grassy area next to a tree. As she looked up at the full moon, someone grabbed her neck from behind. Before she could scream, a hand covered her mouth. Jess struggled to get away, but she was overpowered. Sampson started barking and growling. The person kicked at the dog. Sampson yelped.

An arm held Jess even tighter, and a face was pressed tightly against hers. A man's voice spoke into her ear. "Get in the room."

He held her arm tightly as he dragged her to the room. Her hands were shaking so much that she couldn't get the key card to work. He snatched the key card out of her hand and quickly opened the door. He pushed her inside.

"What do you want?" Jess asked shakily.

"Throw that mutt in the bathroom before I slit its throat."

Jess quickly grabbed Sampson by the collar and led him to the bathroom.

Sampson continued to bark and scratch at the door.

"Keep that mutt quiet, or we're going to have a problem."

Jess opened the bathroom door. "Sampson, NO. Lay."

The dog studied her intently and listened to her orders.

She shut the door behind her and turned around. The goon had a gun strapped to his hip. He was pointing a knife in her direction. "Sit down," he ordered. She looked at him. His greasy dark hair lay lifeless out of the black cap that he was wearing. His facial features were hard, like he'd lived a hard life. She looked into his steely dark eyes, and it felt as though he could see through to her soul.

Shaking, Jess sat down on the edge of the bed. They stared at one another, and she could see the lust in his eyes. Her heart was racing, and she was finding it hard to breathe. Finally, she couldn't stand it any longer. "What do you want?" she asked again.

He sat down and looked at her, running a thumb down the edge of the knife checking the sharpness. "Mr. Easton wants me to give you a message. He wants you to realize that you don't know what you've done, but you will understand soon enough. If you want your husband to live, go home now."

Jess felt like she was kicked in the gut. She licked her lips and nodded her head. "Alright,

I'll go, just please don't hurt us. We'll leave. Daniel will never see us again. I swear."

The man scoffed and stood up. "I don't want to hear your promises. If it were up to me, I would take care of you myself." He walked towards her and pulled her hair back. He ran a finger down her neck.

Jess steeled herself, forcing herself not to move.

He turned and walked back to the table, picking up his knife. Jess closed her eyes trying not to breathe. He came towards her and softly touched her neck with the blade then he pushed the blade harder into her flesh. She whimpered. "I suggest you listen to Mr. Easton. Go home," he said menacingly.

She could feel the tip of the knife slice into her neck. "Please," she begged as she started to cry, "Please, let me go. I'll go home." He pulled the knife away and slipped it into his sheath and turned away.

Jess sat motionless, praying she'd live through this.

He walked to the door, turned the knob, and looked at her one last time. He smiled and said, "I'll be seeing you, Jess."

She sat still on the bed as tears ran down her face, and she started to hyperventilate. Jess put her hand up to her neck and wiped off the trickle of blood that came from the nick. Holding her breath, she waited, hoping he wouldn't come back. After she was sure she was safe, she locked the door, then let Sampson out of the bathroom. Her legs felt weak, and she couldn't control the shaking of her hands.

Sampson jumped on her, smelling her and licking her. His tail was wagging. He turned and started smelling the room where the man had been. He growled and the hair along his back stood up.

Jess frantically began to gather her things and threw them in a bag. She grabbed her keys to leave but stopped. She sat back down on the bed and tried to calm down. She was in no shape to drive. In all honesty, she wasn't sure her legs were even able to walk to her car. They still felt wobbly. The man had scared her, but she needed to think about what she was doing.

She reached into her pants pocket and pulled out the paper with George's number. She punched in his number, hoping he'd answer.

He answered on the second ring. "It's late. What's going on?"

Jess skipped right to the point. "George, they know where I'm at. Daniel's goon was here. He had a gun and a knife. I thought he was going to kill me."

"Whoa Jess, slow down. Are you alright?"

"I don't know," she cried.

"Did they hurt you? Stay there, I'm coming over."

"No, don't come over. I don't want you involved. I'm so sorry I ever opened my mouth. George, I don't know what to do."

"What do you mean?" he asked.

She could feel her eyes tearing up. She stood up and started pacing the room. "Daniel was arrested on what I assume are drug charges. His goon just held a knife to my neck and ordered me to go home, or they'd kill my husband. George, they know it was me behind all of this."

"Stay calm, Jess. It's going to be alright. I told you there might be retaliation. Let's slow down and think this through. Did you get a good look at him?"

Jess let out a long breath. "Yes, I haven't seen this one before. He was wearing a dark cap over dark hair that went to his shoulders. It looked greasy and straggly. He was tall. Maybe 6'2 and muscular. He had rough hands, like he's used to doing hard labor. He had a deep voice."

"Good, that's good, Jess. Now, do you have any idea how they found you?"

"I don't know. I destroyed my phone, just like you told me to. I'm using this burner phone. I've stayed in my room. I haven't gone out except to take Sampson outside."

"Who's Sampson?" George asked.

"My dog. He kicked my dog, George. He threatened to slit his throat. They mean business. They aren't bluffing."

She nervously sat in the chair near Sampson who lay on the floor. "To make matters worse, Peter is representing Daniel in court, and refuses to hear what I have to say."

George listened as Jess repeated the conversation she had had with her husband. When she was finished, the other end of the line was quiet.

"George?"

"Go home. There are too many eyes on him right now, so I think you'll be safe if you just stay away from him. Find out why your husband insists on representing him. It sounds to me like maybe he's being threatened, too. The sting operation went off without a hitch, but unfortunately, Daniel is out of jail until his trial. Try and talk Peter into leaving the state with you. If you want, I'll try and get you guys into witness protection. I'll talk to my buddy on the force and see if he can contact someone in your jurisdiction to keep an eye on things. Jess, whatever you do, don't piss them off."

Jess smiled wryly. "I think it's too late for that. Thanks, George. I can't sleep, so I'm going to head home now."

George's tone took on a deep, serious tone as he said, "Be careful, Jess. These guys don't mess around. They mean business."

They hung up, and Jess looked down at Sampson. "Well, boy, are you ready to go home?"

He stood up and limped to the door. She wished she had listened to Peter when he said to stay out of Daniel's business. Everyone around her was getting hurt. She opened the door and walked to her car, then climbed in and started up the engine.

She dreaded going home. She didn't want to face Peter, and she especially didn't want to see Daniel.

Jess started driving east towards home. Cranking up the radio, she hoped a song would drown out her thoughts. In her rearview mirror she saw Sampson sprawled out on the back seat snoring. Smiling, she focused her attention on the road in front of her and felt herself start to relax.

Following the GPS, she decided that she didn't want to take the thruway back home. Back roads would be safer and she didn't want to take any chances of running into any of Daniel's men. She kept glancing in her mirrors, praying she wouldn't see the black truck following her. So far it had just been her on the road.

Jess followed the route winding around curves and traveling up and down hills bringing her closer to home. The farther she drove the more she began to relax. *Thank goodness I'm the only car on the road,* she thought to herself. She looked at the majestic mountains at dawn and enjoyed their beauty. The pink and blue sky was breathtaking. Huge billowing clouds dotted the sky. As she continued down the road, rolling hills, and creeks drifted by; the leaves on the trees were crimson, yellow, and burnt orange. In another lifetime, she probably would have stopped and taken pictures.

She picked up her phone and glanced at the screen. No one had called. She shouldn't be surprised. No one had her number, except for George and Peter. She scrolled down and found George's number. It was crazy how a complete stranger was the only one she felt safe with.

The phone rang. "Hello?"

"Hi George, it's Jess. I was wondering if you can find any information on Chad and Claudia Wellington. They were the owners of the house we bought. They mysteriously left town, and no one has heard from them since. I'm wondering if there's a connection to Daniel."

"That's an interesting concept," George replied. "I'll get someone to look into it."

Jess smiled. "George, you're the best. I also wanted to tell you that I'm halfway home, and to thank you for all of your--" a curve was coming up, and Jess stepped on her brakes to slow down, but the pedal went all the way to the floor.

"No!" Jess frantically pressed down on the pedal. The car was careening down a winding hill alongside a ravine. "Help!" she yelled as

Sampson stood up and started to bark excitedly. She tried to slow down the car, but nothing worked.

A dump truck was up ahead of her. It was going much slower than her car. She gripped the steering wheel hard and tried to ease the side of her car into the guardrail, hoping it would slow her down. She could hear the screech of metal on metal. She veered back onto the road and kept pushing her foot down on the brake pedal. The dump truck was getting closer. She blew her horn. Nothing helped, he wasn't moving over. She had no choice but to go around him.

She prayed she could keep her car on the road. Her car was speeding closer and closer to the rear of the dump truck. This was not how she wanted to die. Right before she hit the back of the dump truck, she reeled into the next lane, and screamed as she saw a red pickup truck heading straight towards her. She panicked and twisted the car hard to the left. The front of her car hit a guardrail and flipped over it.

Her car tumbled over and over and over until it hit the bottom of the ravine.

Chapter 15

Peter was frantically pacing the halls of the hospital. He had never felt more alone. He ran his hand through his hair and kept glancing hopefully each time he saw a nurse or doctor. Time stood still while Jess was in the operating room. He wished their argument over the phone wasn't the last time he had talked to her. He would give anything to change that.

The worst-case scenario kept running through his mind. He knew when they brought in Jess, it had been bad. Before surgery, the doctors didn't give him a lot of encouragement. Peter looked around at strangers all waiting for news of their loved one. He felt helpless. He found a little chapel and quietly slipped inside. The red carpet and wooden pews took him back to his childhood, when he went to church with his parents. He knelt in a pew and bowed his head. He prayed with all his might that Jess would pull through.

He stepped out of the chapel and walked back towards the surgical waiting room. It wasn't long before a nurse walked out of two large metal doors, exhaustion written all over her face. As she scanned the room, she spotted him sitting in a corner chair nervously tapping his foot. Walking towards him, she took off her mask. Peter couldn't read her face for any indication of how Jess was doing. His palms were sweaty, and his knees felt weak.

"Mr. Stanton, your wife is out of surgery. She's alive, but she's critical."

Peter breathed out a sigh of relief, but it was short lived as the nurse continued, "She has significant swelling in her brain. We won't know how much damage was done until she wakes up. She has suffered a break in her femur. She has several broken ribs and a broken arm on her left side. The next forty-eight hours will be critical."

Peter listened, trying to process what she was telling him, but at the same time, all he could hear was *She's alive.*

When the nurse was finished, Peter cleared his throat and asked, "When can I see her?"

A tall doctor walked over and stood next to the nurse. "We will let you see her, but please understand that we have her in an induced coma so that her body can rest. She's taken a substantial shock, and it may be several weeks before we can bring her out of the coma. Her body needs to heal first."

Peter felt nauseous and dizzy. He couldn't believe this was really happening. He ran his fingers through his hair.

"I understand," he said.

"We'll come and get you from the waiting room when she's out of recovery and into the

ICU. You will only get to see her for a few minutes."

"Thank you," Peter replied.

He sat there, thinking back to what Daniel had said-- that if Peter didn't free him, Jess's life would be in danger. Did he do this? If so, why? Peter had held up his side of the bargain.

The police had taken the car to the station to be examined. So far, based on the evidence of no tire marks on the road, the police suspected that it was a faulty brake line. They weren't treating it like a crime scene. Peter wondered if that would have changed if he had told the police about the threat Daniel had given them. Of course, he wouldn't. He couldn't. He wouldn't take a chance with Jess's life, and if this was a message from Daniel, it was received loud and clear.

"Mr. Stanton?" The nurse brought him back to the present. "You can see her now."

He followed her back to the ICU.

She talked to him in a hushed voice. "The sight of her is going to be a shock. Remember, this is temporary. Please don't touch her, but you can talk to her. You'll have five minutes." She left him as he stood next to his wife's side.

Her head was bandaged, and her face was swollen and bruised. She was on a ventilator. She was so still. If it weren't for all the machines, Peter would have wondered if she was actually alive. His eyes filled with tears. He felt so helpless watching her lie there.

"Jess," Peter whispered, wanting desperately to hold her, but knowing he couldn't. "Please fight to get through this. We have our whole lives together, and I want to spend every last minute of it with you."

The nurse walked in. "Mr. Stanton, I'm sorry, but it's time to leave." He nodded with tears in his eyes and stood back from her bed. He turned one last time to look at his wife. The nurse already had her back to him, checking Jess's monitors and vitals. He walked out of the room, praying they would survive this nightmare.

As Peter was walking towards the elevators, an older, stocky gentleman was walking close behind him. Both men got onto the elevator, and Peter pushed the button for the main floor. Once the elevator started to move, the elderly gentleman pushed the red button, and the elevator stopped.

Peter looked at the man in surprise.

The man held out his hand and said, "I'm George. I know we don't know each other, but I know Jess. She was on the phone with me when she was in the accident, and I called 9-1-1. I know you don't know me, but I'd really appreciate it if you could tell me how she is."

Peter was speechless.

George continued, “Can I take you for a cup of coffee?”

Peter nodded yes. George pushed the button, and the elevator continued down to the main floor. They were silent as they walked out of the hospital.

George looked at Peter. “I noticed that there is a diner right around the corner. Would you like to walk?”

Peter shrugged and put his hands in his pockets. “That would be fine,” he said.

They began walking towards the diner, neither one speaking.

When they reached the diner and were seated at a table, George spoke. “Do you mind if I ask you how she is?”

Peter studied him for a minute. *Who was this man? Why hadn’t Jess ever mentioned him before?*

Peter cleared his throat and crossed his hands on the table. He said, “Would you mind telling me how you know my wife, and why you would be the last one to talk to her?”

A waitress came by with a carafe of coffee. She filled their coffee mugs and laid menus down in front of the men.

Peter handed back the menu. “Just coffee for me.” George did the same.

George looked back at Peter as the waitress walked away. “I’m a private investigator. I’m not sure how much I should be telling you without your wife's permission, but she's kept me apprised of your… ah… situation. I feel it's only right that you know what's going on." He took a sip of coffee. "Your wife hired me to look into Daniel's dealings. She had reason to suspect that he was making and distributing drugs."

Peter swore under his breath. He should have known she couldn't have kept this to herself.

"Why you?" Peter asked.

"I don't understand what you mean," George replied.

"I mean, why did she pick you to help her?"

George nodded. "Ah, I see. Well, she said that she didn't feel safe dealing with the police in town. She thought they might be in Daniel's pocket. She also felt like Daniel had people watching her, following her. She just happened to see my office and called me."

"Where are you from, exactly?" Peter asked.

"Lake George."

"Were you having an affair with my wife, George?"

George laughed and shook his head. "It's purely a business deal."

"Then why would my wife spend days shacked up in a hotel in Lake George and lie to me about it? Why would you be the person she was talking to when she was driving home? Don't lie to me."

George leaned across the table and looked Peter in the eye. "Look, if you don't trust your wife, that's your problem. She was on the phone with me before the accident because she wanted me to look into the previous owners of your house. She thought Daniel might be the one behind the mysterious sale."

"Damn it!" Peter slammed his hand on the table. "Why couldn't she just leave well enough alone?"

George shot back, "Why aren't you helping your wife? Why did she feel like she had to turn to a total stranger? You want to know why she stayed 'shacked up in a hotel', as you say? It's because I asked her to stay put for her own safety. As you recall, that was when Daniel was busted, and it was safer for Jess to not be anywhere near the vicinity."

Peter thought about what the old man had said. George was right. Peter should have taken Jess more seriously. She was stubborn as a mule when she got an idea in her head. He'd known of Jess's suspicions, and he should have shut them down. If he had, things would never have gotten this far.

"Don't tell me anything more," Peter said quickly.

George sat back and glared at Peter. "Look, we don't need to be friends. In fact, I couldn't care less about what you think. I do care about that lady who is fighting for her life in there.

Just tell me how she's doing, and I'll be on my way."

Everything that Peter was trying to juggle was falling to pieces. He wiped his face, exhausted. "I apologize, George. I don't want you to tell me anything because I'm defending Daniel."

"You've got to be kidding me."

"I wish I were. I can't tell you more than that, or I may jeopardize the case, and I can't take that chance. I can, however, tell you about how Jess is doing, and I will let the hospital know that you can visit her once she's out of ICU."

George cleared his throat, looking a little emotional. "Thank you."

Peter nodded. "Right now, it's touch and go with Jess. If you believe in a higher power, then please pray for her. She's got several broken bones and is currently in a medically induced coma."

George shook his head. "Shit, I knew it would be bad. I saw the car at the bottom of the ravine."

Peter sipped his coffee. "It's a miracle she's alive."

"Can I ask you something?" George asked.

"As long as it doesn't have to do with the case," Peter replied.

"Do you think this was an accident?"

Peter thought long and hard about his response. How much could he really trust the old man? How did he know that this guy was even legit? For all he knew, it could be a setup by Daniel.

"Do you have any identification?" Peter asked.

"What?"

"Identification. ID. Something to tell me you are who you say you are."

"Oh. Sure," George replied, pulling out his wallet and showing his private investigator's license.

Peter studied it carefully, and then handed it back. He wiped a hand down his face, then shook his head, praying he was doing the right thing.

"No," Peter said, "I don't think it was an accident. I can't prove it, but it seems too coincidental."

George nodded. "I don't think it was an accident, either. I've got people who can look into this kind of thing. I need to know, and I'm pretty sure Jess would want to know, too."

"As would I." Peter said.

"As would you." George concurred.

"Look, Jess hasn't given me permission to tell you what I know and since you're representing Daniel, I don't think it's a good idea."

"I agree," Peter murmured. "Look, she's my wife. I'd do anything for her."

George looked at Peter and said, "I disagree. If that were true, you wouldn't be defending Daniel."

"I don't have a choice. He threatened to hurt her. I'm not taking any chances."

Peter leaned forward and said, "Look, if you can protect my wife… If you know things that could help put Daniel away, then do it. But please understand, I'm trying to protect her too, and I see no other way out."

George frowned at Peter and said, "The only way to end this is to send Daniel away for a very long time. With attempted murder and the drug charges, we can do that."

Peter shook his head emphatically. "I wish it were that easy. This town has deep pockets, and those pockets are filled by Daniel. Even if he's convicted, his associates will still be out there."

George shook his head "I'm not going to let anyone get away with hurting Jess. I'll see what I can find out about the car."

Peter interrupted, "The police already ruled it an accident."

George continued, "Like I said, I'll see what I can find out about the car. I have connections to certain people who aren't tied to Daniel's pockets. Maybe with any luck, we can work together to put this bastard behind bars. Until then, how do you feel about moving Jess into witness protection? Once she's in the program, we can better protect her."

Peter shook his head. "I don't think that's a good idea. I'm sure you're good at what you do, but I've got to clear him of these charges if I'm going to help Jess. The fewer people who are involved with this case, the better it'll be. George, thanks for all you've done, really, but I think it'll be best if you just go back to Lake George and let me worry about taking care of Daniel. I can't take a chance of getting thrown off this case with Daniel until I know Jess will be safe."

George smiled sadly at Peter. "Peter, the only thing you said that made sense was that I'm good at what I do. You may not want to work together, and that's your prerogative, but that woman lying in that hospital bed deserves answers. Now, you may think you know all the answers, but I highly doubt it."

George stood up and pulled out his wallet. He threw ten dollars on the table to cover the coffees, then turned and walked out the door.

Chapter 16

When Jess opened her eyes, she felt a jolt of pain shoot up her left arm into her neck. The lights were too bright, and she quickly closed them again. She listened to the muffled voices outside of her room. She tried opening her eyes again. It took a few seconds to adjust.

Peter was sitting next to her. Her vision was blurry, but he was smiling and crying at the same time.

He shouted for the doctor, and his voice was so loud it hurt her head. Jess groaned in response, closing her eyes, wanting all the pain to go away. Peter continued saying her name, but it sounded further and further away. Finally, it was quiet, and she could rest.

The next time she woke up, she was more alert, and Peter was once again sitting in the chair beside her, reading a file of papers with a scowl on his face. She tried to move to get more comfortable, and a groan escaped her lips.

Peter turned immediately and grinned widely. He pressed the button for the nurse and said, "Don't move. The nurse will be in soon to give you something for the pain."

"What happened?" Jess croaked. Her mouth felt so dry.

"You were in a car accident."

Jess was quiet as she tried to remember what had happened. It slowly started coming back to her. The argument with Peter. The phone call with George. The brakes. Daniel. Sampson. She looked up at Peter. "Sampson?"

He stroked her hair. "Sampson will be fine. He was thrown from the car and has a broken leg, but he'll be fine."

She let out a sigh of relief, then looked back up at him with tears in her eyes. "What about me?"

He let out a sigh and continued stroking her hair. "You're going to be fine, too. I'm not going to lie; you gave us all quite a scare. Thank God for your seatbelt. You were touch-and-go for a while. But you're going to be just fine."

Jess licked her lips, but her tongue felt like sandpaper. "Water?" she croaked.

A nurse walked into the room. "Jess, it's nice to see you awake. How is your pain?"

"Hurts," Jess responded. "Can I have some water?"

The nurse smiled down at her. "Of course. I'll bring you some just as soon as I take your vitals."

She took Jess's blood pressure and temperature. She recorded the information from the monitors, and showed Jess how to administer pain medication when she needed it.

"I'll be back with your water."

When the nurse left, Jess felt exhausted. She fought to keep her eyes open, but it was no use. She drifted back into a deep sleep.

****

When she woke again, she saw that Peter hadn't moved from her side. "Water?" she asked faintly.

Peter picked up the glass of water and placed a straw in it. He walked over to her and held the glass and straw while she drank. When she was finished, she laid her head back on the pillow. That simple act was exhausting.

She looked at her husband. He looked tired and stressed. His clothes were rumpled, and he looked like he hadn't shaved in a few days.

"How do you feel?" he asked.

"Everything hurts." She pushed the button for more pain relief. "Tell me," she said.

"What do you want to know?" Peter asked.

"What is wrong with me?"

Peter took a deep breath. "You've been in an induced coma for a couple of weeks to give the swelling in your brain time to subside and heal. You have pins in your left leg and your left arm is also broken."

Jess could see tears pooling in Peter's eyes. His voice was getting husky. He squeezed her hand. "You're lucky to be alive."

She tried to process what he'd just told her. The vision of her careening towards the dump truck was vivid in her mind. She *was* lucky to be alive. She began to feel groggy again and tried to stay focused. The pain medications were beginning to work. "Daniel?" she asked as her eyes began to close.

"Don't worry about Daniel. I'll fix this."

****

Peter watched her as she drifted off to sleep. She was sleeping peacefully as he stroked her hair. He thought about Daniel, and how he was supposed to fix this. Her car was unrecognizable at the bottom of the ravine. It was a miracle that she was alive at all. He knew the hole in the brake line wasn't going to be traced back to Daniel, but he knew he was responsible.

He looked back down at the file sitting on an empty chair beside the bed. He picked it up and put it in his briefcase. He clicked it shut and picked up his jacket. With the pain medication administered, he knew he had a few hours before she woke up. He decided to go home and get some sleep. Maybe things would look better when he woke up.

****

When Jess woke again, she found George dozing in the chair beside her. When she shifted to get more comfortable, George's eyes flew open.

She smiled at him. "What are you doing here?" she asked.

"Checking on you," he grumbled. "You scared me half to death!"

She took in a shaky breath. "I was pretty scared, myself. Do you know what happened?"

George nodded. "They're saying it's a faulty brake line. I think it was faulty because someone tampered with it. I have some of my guys checking into it."

Jess lay back on her pillow and thought about what he had said. Somehow, George made her feel safer. "How did you know where to find me?"

George let out a heavy sigh. "Jess, like I said before, I'm very good at what I do. When you were staying at the Star Motel, I put a tracker on your car. We were on the phone when you had the accident. I phoned the coordinates in to the sheriff's office and called all the hospitals in the vicinity until I found you."

Jess started to close her eyes. She asked, "Did you find anything out about the former owners of our house?"

George shook his head. "You almost died, but you're still not letting this go, are you?" He let out a weary breath. "No, not yet, but I've got people working on it. I'll let you know once I find out something." George looked down at his watch. "I've gotta get going. I just wanted to see you for myself and make sure you're going to be alright."

Jess opened her eyes and gave him a small smile. "Thanks, George. For everything. I mean it." He nodded, and left the room.

A few hours later, Peter came back. Jess was sitting up, eating dinner.

"You don't know how happy I am that you're up and eating. When you were in a coma, I didn't know if you were ever going to open those beautiful green eyes again." He sat down next to her and held her hand. "I love you so much. I'm so grateful that you're alive." He delicately pushed her hair up away from her face. "We're going to get through this, Jess. I promise."

She smiled sadly. "I'm sorry I wasn't honest with you."

He shook his head. "Let's not talk about that right now. Just concentrate on getting better."

She tried to nod, but a pain shot up through her neck. "How's Sampson? Is he home yet?"

He smiled. "Yes, he is. He's still pretty banged up, but he's home. Don't worry, I'm taking good care of him for you. The vet said something strange, though."

She looked up at him. "What's that?"

"They found a GPS tracker implanted under his skin. Would you happen to know anything about that?"

"No. Are you sure?"

Peter nodded. "I'm sure. I even have it in a baggy at home."

Jess took a sip of tea and leaned back against the mattress on the bed. "I bet that's how Daniel and his goons knew where I was. That has to be it. I thought it was my phone, but Sampson was always with me. That has to be it, Peter."

Peter nodded. "I agree. I think it was their way of keeping tabs on you."

They were both quiet for a minute, then Peter cleared his throat. "Jess, I think it would be best if you disappeared for a while until after the trial. Daniel is a dangerous man, and he's obviously out for revenge. Maybe go to your parents or back to North Carolina, somewhere that's not here. I would feel better if it was far from here." Jess opened her mouth in astonishment, then closed it, then opened it one more time. "I can't leave. Where would I go? They'll find me. You know they will. Let me help you put him away. He belongs in jail."

Peter turned towards her, his eyes the color of gray steel. He ran a frustrated hand through his hair, then turned and started pacing the room.

"I told you, Jess, I'm not putting him away. I'm representing him."

She looked at him, astounded. "You've got to be kidding me. Peter, he's a drug dealer! He kills people for a living. You know he's behind this. Even if they can't prove it, you know he's behind my accident."

Peter stood up, agitated. "Don't you think I know that?" he hissed. "He's got ties in this community that go deep. He's connected to almost everything in this town. He's told me that if I don't keep him out of jail, he's going to kill you. I don't have a choice. That's why you have to leave. That's the only way I know how to keep you safe. You almost died, Jess. It's a miracle that you didn't. I won't take that chance again."

She glared angrily. "He already tried to kill me. You said yourself it's a miracle that I survived. Yet here you are, telling me you're going to defend him."

He took a deep breath, which Jess knew was his way of trying to calm down. He sat down on her bed and took her hand. "Do I think he had someone tamper with the brake line? Yes. That could have gone all sorts of ways. You would have had an accident, but it could have been a fender-bender or running off the road and hitting the guardrail. It didn't have to be as catastrophic as it actually was. I think it was meant as a warning to show me he was serious."

Jess wrestled with what he was telling her. Part of her wanted to believe him. She took in his disheveled look, and she could see the worry on his face. This conversation wasn't over, not by a long shot. But she was tired, and she was worried about Peter. She'd let it go for now.

Peter leaned over and kissed the top of her head, then stroked her hair. "Honey, I'm sorry. Let's not worry about this right now. We'll talk about it later." He looked down at his watch. "Visiting hours are almost over. I'll let you get some sleep, and I'll come and see you in the morning."

Jess smiled sadly. "I'll see you in the morning."

He stood up and put the papers in his briefcase. He slipped on his coat, then leaned over and kissed her. He smoothed back her hair. "You are my world, Jess. I'm not going to let anything happen to you. No one knows about this except for us and Daniel."

For an instant, Jess thought about telling him about George, and how he was still looking into the case. George also thought Daniel's goons had something to do with the brake line. Maybe he could help her, because obviously Peter was going to defend Daniel whether she liked it or not.

"I'll get Daniel off. I don't know how, but I'll figure it out, and I swear he'll pay for what he's done. He won't get away with trying to kill you. Just don't tell anyone anything, and I promise that we'll figure this out together."

She had pressed the button to help her with the pain, and it was making her drowsier. She fought to keep her eyes open. He kissed her again and left as she drifted off to sleep.

Chapter 17

It had been three weeks, and David was no closer to finding any information. The DA was staying close-mouthed about this case, as was the Attorney General. The only information he'd received was that the person who tipped them off was anonymous. Hell, most people who narked on a drug dealer were anonymous, unless they were an undercover cop. There was nothing about where the person was from, or whether it was a man or a woman. He was going to have to do a little investigating of his own if he was going to save his hide.

He didn't consider himself a "bad cop." He didn't go around harassing others or going after innocent people. He liked his quiet little town. Daniel had helped to fund his campaign when he ran for sheriff. In exchange, David looked the other way when "packages" were hauled out from Daniel's shed. Sure, he knew what those packages consisted of, but they had an agreement. As long as the drugs weren't distributed in his town, then what was the harm?

Daniel took care of this town. When the public park needed an upgrade, Daniel took care of it. When the town needed a new ambulance, the funds became available through an anonymous donor. No questions asked. The arrangement benefited everyone. But now, if the state attorney general looked into the going's on in this town, she might think otherwise. That wouldn't be good for David, the mayor, or anyone else.

David grabbed the keys off his desk and put on his hat. He walked outside and down the sidewalk towards Peter's office. He wanted to know the latest about Daniel's case. Maybe some information had come to light that David could use.

He groaned when he saw the closed sign hanging in the window. Once again, he'd be driving to Peter's house. It would be more private there, anyway. Maybe that would be for the best.

He smiled to himself when he saw Peter's truck sitting in the driveway. He parked his car and walked up onto the porch. He rang the doorbell.

In a matter of seconds, Peter swung the door open. David was surprised at Peter's appearance. It looked as though he hadn't slept in days. His eyes looked bloodshot, and his hair didn't look like it had been combed in a week. His clothes were wrinkled and looked as though they had been slept in.

"Hi, David," Peter said, squinting into the sunlight. "To what do I owe the pleasure?"

David cleared his throat. "Are you okay? You don't look so well. Are you sick? I was surprised to see the closed sign on the door of your office."

Peter looked like he carried the weight of the world on his shoulders. It almost looked as though there might be tears in his eyes, but David couldn't be sure. Peter let out a heavy sigh. "I'm okay."

He moved back to let David into the house. "Don't mind the mess. Between Jess being in the hospital and Daniel's case, I haven't had much time to tidy up."

David looked around at the pile of dishes in the sink and mugs scattered throughout the house. "How is Jess doing?" David asked.

"She's getting stronger each day. In fact, if everything goes well, she'll be coming home from the hospital soon."

"That's great news," David said with a smile.

Peter remained grim. "She still has a long way to go. She was in bad shape when they pulled her from the ravine. It's a miracle she's still alive."

David sat down in a chair. "At least she's alive, Peter. That's what's important."

Peter poured two cups of coffee and sat down at the table across from David.

David scanned the papers and folders scattered between them. "How are things going with Daniel's trial?"

Peter put down his cup and shook his head. "I don't know. I managed to keep him out of jail until his trial, but the DA hasn't given me much to go on. I know about as much as what they said on the news. We can't deny that drugs were confiscated from his property, because that's become public record. All I can really do is get him a plea agreement to try and keep him out of jail, but he won't go for it. He seems to think he'll be declared innocent when this is all over."

"Is there anything I can do?" David asked. "I'd still be happy to help with the case if I can."

Peter looked at him for a minute as though pondering the question. "Actually, yes. I'm going to try and get him off on a technicality if I can. I've requested the documents from the DEA, but I haven't received anything yet. Do you think you can poke around and see if there's anything we can use?"

David smiled. "I'll look into it today." He took another sip of coffee, then said, "By the way, what did they determine was the cause of Jess's accident?"

Peter stood up and carried his mug to the sink. "As of right now, it looks like it was a hole in the brake line. They're ruling it as an accident."

David studied Peter. "Something is telling me you don't believe that. What's going on?"

Peter was quiet for a moment. Then he looked at David and shrugged. "I'm sure it was an accident. You just wonder how these things happen, you know?"

"I know," David replied. "As a police officer, you respond to all sorts of horrific accidents, and you wonder how something so terrible could happen. I'm glad she's going to be alright." He looked at his watch. "Well, I best be heading back to the office. I'll let you know what I find out with the DEA. Give Jess my best when you see her." He stood up and let himself out.

****

David waited until visiting hours were over before he went in to see Jess. He didn't want to bump into Peter, but he wanted to find out what Jess knew. His senses were telling him that Jess knew more than she was letting on.

He waited until the nurses' station was empty, then walked past it into Jess's room, holding a small bouquet of flowers. He quietly walked over and pushed her pain medication dispenser.

****

Jess opened her eyes and was startled when she saw David standing next to her. Her hands automatically started combing through her hair.

He cleared his throat and smiled. “I wanted to check on the town’s newest resident. How are you doing?”

He placed the bouquet on the counter and sat in the chair beside her.

She winced as she raised her head in order to see him better. “I’m feeling better than I did. There’s going to be a lot of physical therapy in my future, but I’m alive.”

“I’m really glad to hear that. You gave everyone quite a scare. Is there anything I can get for you?”

Jess nodded. “I’d love some water.”

He lifted the pitcher of water and poured some in a cup.

She adjusted her bed and tried to maneuver her body into a sitting position. He placed a straw in the water and handed it to her, then waited for her to finish before taking the cup away.

“So, how are you doing?”

She smiled sadly. “I’m pretty banged up but getting a little better each day.”

He patted her hand. “I’m glad to hear it.”

There was a moment of silence before he spoke again. “Jess, I looked at the evidence concerning your car.”

Jess was trying hard to concentrate. She was feeling really out of it. “Yes, I heard… I heard… it was ruled as… as an accident. I believe they said it was a faulty… faulty… brake line."

David nodded in agreement. "That's what they say, but I've got my doubts. Is there anyone who would want to hurt you?"

Jess looked at him, unsure of what to say.

He continued. "You're safe with me. I'm a police officer, and I want to make sure that whoever did this won't get away with it."

Jess knew better than to tell him the whole story, but she couldn't remember why. She shrugged her shoulders. "It's over with. Whoever did this got… got their message across loud… loud and clear." Hopefully, David would relay that message to Daniel.

David kept digging. "It was Daniel, wasn't it? He was the one behind this

She studied him, surprised to hear him say that. She still had that nagging feeling that she couldn't trust him. She was feeling groggy, and it was an effort to keep her eyes open. Daniel already knew it was her. The DEA knew it was her, and eventually, Peter would find out as well.

Her eyes filled with tears. "Daniel's mad at me… he knows I'm the one who told. He knows, and he's mad."

"Jess, do you have any proof it was Daniel? I want to protect you. It's my job and I take my job very seriously."

Her eyes kept closing, but he was still talking.

He leaned closer to her. "Who else knows about this? Think, Jess, it's important. I want to protect you, and anyone else who may be involved."

She thought about George, but once again, she had a nagging feeling not to mention him, so she said, "No one. Not even Peter."

Jess closed her eyes. She felt so groggy, so out of it. She was tired.

"Get some rest," he said.

"Good night, David."

****

The next morning, David drove to the district attorney's office. Everyone in this county was in Daniel's pocket, including the DA. He was sure he could work out a deal on Daniel's behalf.

David marched into the DA's office and strode up to the secretary's desk.

"Is he in?" David asked.

"He's on the phone, but he should be off soon. Have a seat."

David sat, thinking about how he was going to clean up this mess. Why couldn't people just mind their own business and leave well enough alone? If it wasn't for that nosy bitch, none of this would be happening right now. If her brakes went out on the way home from Lake George and she had died in the ravine, she'd be out of the way and no longer a liability. He was sure Daniel had put the order out to put that hole in Jess's brake line."

The door opened.

"David, what can I do for you?"

"Thanks for seeing me, Melvin," David said, standing and walking towards the office.

The door to the office closed, and the two men sat down.

David felt uncomfortable in the plush leather seat. He always hated these chairs. He looked at the district attorney and said, "I suppose you heard about Daniel."

Melvin nodded. "I have. It's quite a mess he's got himself into."

David agreed. "He wants us to make this go away."

Melvin leaned back in his chair and let out a heavy sigh. "I'm not so sure that's going to be easy to do."

"I didn't say it was going to be easy. I said Daniel wants this to go away."

"I'll see what I can do. I might be able to make some of the evidence disappear." He made air quotes with his fingers when he said 'disappear'. "I don't know how much it'll help, though."

"What do you mean?" David asked.

"With the amount of money and drugs that were confiscated at the scene, this has gotten the attorney general's attention. Audrey has extra security set up around the evidence. She's set her mind to making Daniel an example to others like him and putting him away for a long time. Like I said, I'll do what I can, but I can only reach so far."

David looked at Melvin. "This whole thing can blow up in a real bad way."

Melvin stood up, signaling that the meeting was over. "Is there anything else?" he asked in a measured voice.

David stood up. "Do what you can. I'll try and keep Daniel off our asses."

Chapter 18

So many secrets, so many lies. That was what was going through Jess's head when she woke up that morning. It was Tuesday, and the first morning in a month that she was finally waking up in her own bed. It felt great to be home again. It would have been better if she didn't live next door to the man who had put her in the hospital to begin with. She still didn't have absolute proof that it was him, but she knew in her heart that it was.

She stood up. It took her longer to get dressed with her injuries. She wished her body was fluid again, but right now, it was rigid and still healing, especially her leg. She could smell bacon coming from down the hall. She grabbed her cane and walked towards the smell.

Peter turned around and smiled at her. "You look beautiful. Have a seat, breakfast is ready."

Jess pulled out the chair and sat down. "Aren't you going to be late for work?" she asked.

He shrugged. "It's your first morning home. I wanted to make you breakfast before I left." He looked at her skeptically. "Are you sure you're going to be alright by yourself?"

She smiled at him confidently and said, "I'm fine, really. I'm going to check my emails and start back to work. I'm sure there will be tons to get caught up on. By the way, how's the case coming along?"

He took a mug of coffee and sat down across from her. For the first time, she noticed how much weight he had lost. He looked tired--no, "tired" wasn't the word she would use to describe him. "Exhausted" was more like it. He looked like he carried the weight of the world on his shoulders, and in a way, he did.

She reached across the table and held his hand. Their eyes met. "I'm sorry this is happening. Believe me, if I could turn back time and do things differently, I would."

He shook his head. "No, you wouldn't. Once you make up your mind, there's no changing it. I warned you to stay out of Daniel's business, but you didn't." He must have seen that she was getting angry and softened his voice. He put a hand on her shoulder. "Look, I know how broken you were when Jason died. I know how passionate you are about ridding the world of those who seek to destroy other people but look at what it cost us."

She hastily wiped away a tear. "Who knew that living in the middle of nowhere would be more dangerous than living in the city?"

Peter let out a wry smile. "Next time, we pick out the house together, and we do a thorough background check on who our neighbors are."

He looked at his watch and stood up. “I’ve got to get to work. I love you.”

As he left, Sampson came limping into the kitchen and put his head on Jess’s leg. “Sampson, I am so glad to see you.” Her eyes filled with tears. “I honestly didn’t think we would survive that,” she whispered. Her hand ran across his back, and she could feel the scar from the incision where they had removed the GPS tracker. “There isn’t anyone that Daniel hasn’t tried to destroy in our family, is there, boy?” He let out a whine, and Jess knew he needed to be let out. She used her cane to stand up, and they both walked out into the yard.

It was nice to be in the fresh air. The sun was shining, and although it was cool outside, it felt refreshing. The leaves were mostly off the trees. If she was healthy, she probably would have enjoyed raking them up, but this year, they would stay where they were.

Jess heard a truck coming down the road. Her heart sped up and her breathing was shallow. She looked in the direction it was coming from and saw that it was the truck that had been following her when she went to Lake George. She froze. It drove past Daniel’s house and continued to her house. When it reached her house, it slowed down. She could see Daniel’s goons watching her. They waved to her, and then sped off down the road.

She looked over towards Daniel's house, thankful that he wasn't standing there staring in her direction, watering his lawn. Jess still couldn't believe he was back out on the streets, but the wheels of justice sometimes turned in a way she didn't understand. While she was outside, she noticed how quiet it was. It felt almost eerie. There were no more box trucks pulling up to the shed. She wondered if he had moved his drug business somewhere else, or if he was just biding his time.

She knew why Peter was defending him, but that didn't mean she couldn't hope he'd still be put behind bars. They could always move. That's probably what the last owners did. When this was over, that's what she wanted to do.

Sampson came limping up to Jess, and they hobbled back into the house. Thinking of the previous owners, she pulled out her cell phone and dialed George's number.

He picked it up on the second ring. "Hello?"

"George, it's Jess. How are you?"

"Jess! It's so good to hear your voice. How are you feeling?"

"I'm doing better than the last time you saw me. I'm home now."

"That's progress. So, to what do I owe the pleasure?"

She leaned back on the couch. "I was wondering if you found out any information about the previous owners?"

George let out a deep sigh. "I wish I did. It seems like they just disappeared into thin air. There's no missing person's report. I've tried to find extended family, looked through death certificates, court records, property sales, but I haven't found anything. It's possible they could be in witness protection. I have a friend in the bureau who's going to look into it for me."

"Thanks, George. I don't know what I'd do without you."

"Has Daniel still been threatening you?"

"No, it's been quiet. I think he's keeping to himself, or at least, I hope so. His goons drove past my house sending their message, but there's nothing I can do. They aren't trespassing, and they aren't doing anything that I can use against them."

"How's the trial going?" George asked.

Jess took a glass out of the cabinet and filled it with ice water. She walked over to the table and sat down. "We don't discuss it. What Daniel tells Peter is confidential, and since Peter knows what I've done, he refuses to tell me anything. Say, did anything ever come from your friend looking at my brake line?"

"No, sorry. There was definitely a hole in the brake line, but we can't tell definitively if it was tampered with. Unfortunately, Daniel is very smart. Be careful, Jess."

She looked out the window towards Daniel's house. "I will. Let me know what else I can do to bring him down."

The line was silent for a moment before George spoke. "Jess, I think you should step back from this. He's dangerous and powerful. I'll keep working on it, but I think you should stop. Let this go."

She couldn't believe what she was hearing. She stood up with the help of her cane and paced the living room. "George, I can't just walk away. The man is psychotic. He tried to kill me. After all he's done to me, I'm not just going to quietly go away. He needs to be put behind bars for a very, very long time, and I'll do whatever it takes to make that happen."

George groaned. "Just think about it, Jess. That's all I'm asking."

The phone call ended. Jess sank down on the couch, and Sampson put his head on her lap. She petted him, thinking about how Daniel had turned her life completely upside down. She was frustrated. How could George think she could just walk away? She knew she was at a disadvantage. She didn't really know how to defend herself. She didn't own a gun. She had never taken any self-protection classes. She needed to change that.

She opened up her laptop, typed in "martial arts" and looked for a class in the next town over. She didn't trust this town. The town that owed Daniel their very existence. There weren't many people in this town that somehow didn't have a tie to Daniel in some way. She wasn't willing to sell her soul.

Jess jumped when the doorbell rang. She startled easily since coming back here. Closing her laptop, she peered out the window. Victoria was standing at the door. She really, really didn't want to see anyone, but her curiosity got the best of her. With a deep breath, she stood and opened the door.

"Hello, Victoria."

Jess was surprised at how different Victoria appeared. Her eyes were hollow. Her skin color was pale. Her hair lay limp. She had lost weight. She looked awful.

Victoria's eyes met Jess's. After a moment of silence, Jess noted Victoria's strained smile as she said, "Hi, Jess. I know this is probably a bad idea, but I couldn't stand not knowing how you are."

Jess stood rigid. "Did Daniel send you here?"

"No, he's in town meeting with Peter about the case. He doesn't know that I'm here." She looked around nervously, then asked, "So, how are you?"

"I'm fine."

They stood silently watching each other. Victoria nervously pushed up her long sleeves, then quickly pulled them down again. It wasn't quick enough. Jess could see the purple bruise along her lower arm. It was about the size of a hand. Jess wondered if there was a matching bruise on her other arm. She didn't ask. Instead, she asked, "Would you like to come in?"

Victoria nodded and stepped inside. They walked towards the kitchen table.

"Coffee?" Jess offered.

"That would be great," Victoria said.

As Jess made coffee, Victoria studied the kitchen. "I love what you did with the place. It feels so peaceful here."

Jess bit her tongue and tried to refrain from saying something about Daniel making it anything but peaceful.

Victoria continued talking. "Daniel doesn't know that I'm here."

Jess eyed her warily. "So you've already said. How can you be sure?"

Victoria lifted her hand to push some hair behind her ear. Her hand was shaking.

"Victoria, is everything okay?"

Victoria's eyes filled with tears. "I'm so sorry, Jess. None of this should have happened."

Jess came over and put a mug of coffee in front of her. She wasn't ready to let Victoria off the hook because of a few tears. "Did you know about the drugs?"

Victoria let out a sob and wiped away her tears. "Yes, and I'm not going to pretend I didn't. I didn't agree with it. I tried to confront

Daniel about it once, but--" She stopped, then forced herself to continue. "Well… you know his temper."

Jess remained silent, watching Victoria struggle.

"I tried to reason that he was using the money to help the town. That he was taking something bad and turning it into something good." She looked into Jess's eyes. "I know it sounds screwed up, but hey, we're all screwed up in some way, right? No one was getting hurt. At least, not until now."

Jess sipped her coffee and thought about what Victoria was saying. She thought about the bruise. She could see the fear in Victoria's eyes. She knew about Daniel's temper. And as much as she hated to admit it, she believed Victoria.

Jess finally spoke. "What happened to the previous owners of this house?"

Victoria shook her head. "I honestly don't know." She looked down at her watch. "It's almost time for Daniel to come home. I've got to go. Thanks for the coffee."

"Wait, Victoria, please. Don't go back there. It's not safe, and you know it. I'll help you. Peter will help you."

Victoria looked at her sadly. "Jess, I'm fine. Daniel has a temper, yes, but he's good to me. Without him, I wouldn't have The Blooming Boutique. I have so much because of him. I don't want to start over. I think it's best if we weren't friends anymore."

Jess studied her. "Best for who? You, or Daniel?"

Victoria met Jess's eyes. "Both. I just wanted to make sure you're alright. I see that you are, so I'll be going. Please, Jess, drop it."

Jess was disappointed knowing that she wasn't going to change Victoria's mind. "Alright, if that's what you want, I'll drop it. I hope you and Daniel will be very happy together."

Victoria nodded and turned to leave.

Jess was dejected at this turn of events but wasn't completely surprised. She thought back to their lunches and jogs. She'd seen some of the bruises, and she knew there were many she had not. She did know that unless someone wanted help and was willing to seek help, there wasn't much she could do for her friend. Jason had taught her that lesson the hard way.

Chapter 19

Sampson stood up and licked Jess's hand. He wanted to go out. Jess groaned as she threw back the blanket and crawled out of bed. She opened the door and let him out. He was trained enough not to worry about being outside alone. He walked outside, and then stopped. His head turned towards Daniel's house. He started barking.

"Sampson, NO!" Jess hissed, not wanting to wake up Peter.

The barking continued, and Sampson started running towards Daniel's house. Jess groaned. This wasn't going to be good, but she wasn't going to risk something bad happening to Sampson.

She hobbled inside and threw a jacket over her pajamas.

Peter roused from his sleep. "What are you doing?" .

"Going to Daniel's and getting Sampson," Jess said in a rush.

She limped out of the room to slip on her shoes next to the door. Peter quickly climbed out of bed and followed her.

"No, Jess, you're not. You're in no shape to go anywhere. Sampson will come back. Come on to bed."

She slipped on her shoes, then looked up at him. "Yes, Peter, I am. Now, you can choose to go back to bed, or you can come with me. It's your choice, but you'd better hurry up if you are going with me."

Peter threw back the blanket and grumbled, "Just give me a minute to get changed."

He turned and walked back to their room. Jess couldn't wait, she had a bad feeling about this. Grabbing a flashlight and her cane, she let herself out the front door. She hobbled across their yard as quickly as she was able and saw Sampson barking wildly outside of Daniel's house.

"Sampson, come!" Jess ordered, but Sampson just kept pacing and barking.

A blood-curling scream rang out. It was Victoria.

Jess banged on the door. "Victoria, let me in!" She could hear Daniel shouting at his wife. She heard glass breaking and tried the doorknob. It was locked. "Victoria!" she screamed again.

Sampson was jumping and barking, going out of his mind. She had to do something.

She heard Peter call after her: "Jess, don't you dare go in there."

She looked at her husband, and wondered if he knew her at all. Racing to the back door, she tried the back doorknob. "Shit," she mumbled. It was also locked. Jess wildly scrambled for something to help her break in. She heard Victoria scream again. Her heart was racing as she ran over to the flower garden and picked up a big rock that was being used as part of the border. Hurling it through the glass window of the living room door, she braced herself as glass shards went flying every which way. Pieces of glass embedded in her hair, pushed against her scalp. Jess slid off her jacket and wrapped it around her hand, pushing the jagged edges away. Dropping her jacket to the ground, she reached in and unlocked the door. She hastily pulled her arm out, and Peter grabbed it.

"Jess, don't."

She wrenched her arm away. "Don't touch me!"

Jess hobbled inside. She could hear screaming coming from upstairs. Sampson shot ahead of her as she made her way up the stairs. She could hear frantic barks along with Daniel yelling at the dog. A moment later, Sampson cried out in pain, and Jess knew that Daniel was going to destroy everything in his path. When she finally arrived at the dimly lit room, Victoria was lying on the bed in a fetal position, crying and covering her head. Daniel stood over Victoria, fist clenched, ready to punch her again.

"You son of a bitch!" Jess screamed as she staggered towards Daniel and pushed him away.

He whirled around, grabbed her by the throat, and pushed her up against the wall. "I should have killed you when I had the chance," he seethed.

Sampson growled and snapped at Daniel, grabbing his pant leg and pulling. Daniel kicked off the dog, and Sampson went skidding towards the bed.

Jess gasped for breath as Daniel began to smile.

"Well, well, well, look who's here, darling. It's your good friend, Jess."

Jess could hear Victoria sobbing as she continued to struggle to breathe, unsuccessfully trying to pull his hands away. Her lungs burned and she felt dizzy. She quickly lifted her good knee and kneed him between the legs. Daniel doubled over in surprise.

She turned away from him, gasping for breath. Sampson ran to Jess, barking and whining. Her bad leg gave out and she sank to the floor. Sampson began licking her face.

Daniel kicked the dog, sending him across the floor. Standing over her, Daniel pulled her up by her hair. "You stupid bitch."

As he brought back his arm to punch her in the face, a dark figure lunged towards Daniel, knocking him to the floor with a thud. She screamed and dragged herself over against the wall. Sampson barked wildly. Victoria was still sobbing.

She focused her eyes on the figure and was shocked to see it was Peter who had tackled

Daniel to the ground. The men were rolling, fists flying in all directions. Daniel rolled over on top of Peter and started pummeling him as Peter lay helpless.

"Stop!" Jess shouted, rushing over to help Peter. Before she could reach the two men, Victoria's voice rang out.

"Stop it!" Victoria screamed. "Just stop it!"

A gunshot rang out, and everyone stopped. The smell of gun powder was pungent in the air, and pieces of plaster had fallen from the ceiling where the bullet had punched through. Jess's ears rang as she watched Victoria holding the gun in both hands, pointing it back and forth between Jess and Daniel. Tears mixed with blood were streaming down her face, giving her a grotesque look.

Daniel stood up, and Peter slowly sat up and moved to Jess's side.

Daniel smiled. "Victoria, honey," he said calmly. "Nice work, now give me the gun."

Victoria looked at him, still sobbing. Her right eye was swollen shut. She wiped her face with one hand, smearing the blood that was coming from her nose.

"Stop!" she ordered pointing the gun at Daniel. "Don't take a step closer. Look at me, Daniel. You did this. You did this to me! Why? Why did you do this to me?"

Daniel continued to look calm and walked toward her.

She pulled the hammer of the revolver back and yelled, "Stay right there!"

Jess could see Daniel's jaw clench. "Give me the gun, Victoria."

She aimed the gun at Daniel's chest. "I said, stay right there."

She turned the gun on Jess. "And you!" she shouted, "You should have just minded your own business, and this would never have happened. I told you to stop. Why couldn't you just stop?"

"Victoria," Jess said calmly. "I can help you." She looked at Peter. "*We* can help you. Just put down the gun."

Victoria looked from Daniel to Peter to Jess. Daniel lunged towards Victoria, trying to grab the gun.

"No!" screamed Jess. Sampson barked wildly. A shot rang out.

Both Daniel and Victoria fell to the ground, with Daniel on top.

Jess turned her head and looked at them both lying motionless on the floor. The smell of metal wafted through her nostrils as blood began to pool on the floor below the two bodies.

"Victoria!" she shouted. "Victoria, wake up!" She stood up and walked towards the bodies. She shoved Daniel off of her friend and saw a hole in his chest. "Please tell me he's dead," she cried.

"Oh, he's dead alright," said a voice behind them. They both turned to see David, still holding his semiautomatic.

"You? You shot Daniel?" Jess asked, bewildered.

David raised his eyebrows. "I didn't have much of a choice."

Jess gazed at Victoria. Her friend looked so pale, so lifeless.

"Victoria?" Jess asked David in a shaky voice. "Is she dead, too?"

David didn't answer her, and instead began calling on his radio, requesting an ambulance and back up. He walked over to Daniel.

Jess began shaking her head back and forth. "No, no, no," she said. "You said he's dead. Let him be dead. Don't help--"

David knelt down and put his fingers to Daniel's wrist.

Jess began to run towards David to push him away from Daniel, but Peter grabbed her arm and pulled her back. "David, stop!" Jess yelled.

He looked up at Jess. "No pulse," he said.

David then began to check Victoria's vitals.

"Is she alive?" Jess asked.

David looked up. "Yes, she's alive. Her vitals are weak, but she's alive."

"Thank God," she stammered, as she collapsed against Peter.

The sound of sirens grew louder and came to a stop in front of the house. Blue and red lights bounced off the walls, adding a new dimension to the chaos.

****

The paramedics entered the room and began assessing Daniel and Victoria.

Victoria lay on the floor unmoving. Jess stood next to Peter, helplessly watching.

"Victoria, please wake up," Jess said over and over again. "Victoria, it's over. You can wake up from this horrible, horrible dream."

Still, Victoria lay motionless. Jess could see the rise and fall of her chest and was relieved to see that she was breathing. Daniel had beaten her terribly. The amount of blood pooled around her body was alarming. Jess hoped it was Daniel's and not Victoria's.

David stood back as both Daniel and Victoria were taken out of the room.

Jess started shaking now that this nightmare was over. Peter pulled a blanket off the bed and wrapped it around her shoulders.

Jess looked at David. "Was Victoria shot, too?

David shook his head. "No, she's going to hurt, especially when she hit the floor under Daniel, but no, she wasn't shot."

"But there was so much blood." Jess's teeth were starting to chatter.

He put his hand on her shoulder. "She's going to be alright, Jess."

"How did you know to come?"

"Peter called me and told me that something was going on at Daniel's, and that I needed to come right away."

Jess shuddered. "I'm glad you did."

Now that the adrenaline rush was over, her body was starting to ache. Her leg throbbed, and she felt weak. She leaned into Peter.

David studied her. "Do you need a ride to the hospital? You don't look so good."

Jess shook her head no. "I just saw a man die and my friend battered and bruised. I'll be alright. I just want to go home."

David patted her on the back.

Peter put a hand on David's shoulder. "If there's an internal investigation, I will help in any way I can."

David shook hands with Peter. "Thanks, I appreciate it."

Jess looked up at Peter. "Thank you for believing me. I don't know what would have happened if you hadn't."

Peter wrapped Jess in his arms and said, "I'm glad I did, too. Jess, I know you thought you were doing the right thing, but the right thing almost got you killed."

Jess pulled away. "How can you say that? The right thing saved Victoria's life. The right thing got a thug off the streets. The right thing just got *you* out of defending a maniac, but let's not mention that."

She limped out through the door and left Peter standing alone.

Chapter 20

Victoria looked unrecognizable when Jess stood in the doorway of her hospital room. She had a broken arm and a few broken ribs. Her face was swollen from where she had been punched numerous times, and the space underneath her eyes were beginning to turn bright purple.

Jess's heart broke for her friend. She wiped away her tears and walked inside the room.

Standing at the edge of the bed she said, "Oh, Victoria. I'm so sorry this happened to you."

Victoria could barely open her left eye and sounded hoarse when she spoke. "Why couldn't you just stay away?"

Jess couldn't believe what she heard. Surely, she was mistaken. "What did you say?" she asked quietly.

Victoria tried to speak louder. "Why couldn't you just stay away?"

Jess was stunned, trying to process what Victoria had just said. "Victoria, I was trying to help you. You would have died if I hadn't come in when I did."

Victoria tried to shake her head, but it was in a brace. She closed her eyes. "I could have survived it. It would have been over. Life would have gone on."

Jess was shocked. Victoria couldn't actually believe what she was saying. "You could have been killed. Don't you get that?"

Jess could hear the bitterness in Victoria's voice when she said, "You don't know me. You don't know my life. Don't presume a situation that you know nothing about. Where's my husband? Where's Daniel?"

Jess swallowed hard, and gently held onto Victoria's hand. "Victoria, he's dead. Daniel is dead. He can't hurt you anymore."

Victoria let out an anguished wail. "No! Please tell me you're lying! He can't be dead!"

Jess listened to her friend sob for her dead husband and felt helpless.

When Victoria was calmer, she asked quietly, "Did I… Did I kill him?"

"What? No! You didn't kill him."

"But… but… the last thing I remember was him coming towards me for the gun and I was terrified."

Jess sat on the edge of Victoria's bed. "No, you didn't shoot him. He was coming towards you, but David got there just in time. David shot him."

Victoria squeezed her eyes shut. "No, no, no. Please tell me this is all a bad dream."

Everything that Jess said was wrong. How could this be so wrong? Surely Victoria should be relieved that Daniel was dead. She wouldn't be abused any longer. How could she not see that?

Jess let go of Victoria's hand. "It's finally over. Don't you get that? You don't have to hide the bruises anymore. You're free of him. He's gone."

Victoria was still crying. Jess handed her a tissue, feeling awkward.

Jess cleared her throat and tried again. "Victoria, would you like me to leave?"

"No," she whispered. "I don't want to be alone. Not now. Not ever. Can you do me a favor, though?"

"Sure," Jess replied, relieved. Maybe Victoria had come to her senses. "What is it?"

Victoria whispered softly, "Don't say anything else. Just be here."

Jess smiled through her tears and did as Victoria asked. She sat there while Victoria slept. At times, she heard Victoria whimper and knew she must be reliving the nightmare of what had become her life.

Jess closed her eyes and tried to relax while Victoria slept, but she kept seeing Daniel and the look of hatred on his face. She couldn't get the vision out of her mind of blood oozing from Victoria's head as she held the gun. The look of triumph in Daniel's eyes when he thought he was going to kill Jess.

Peter walked in the room, and set down a flower bouquet with a bright blue balloon that said, "Get Well Soon." "How is she doing?" he asked.

"The doctors say she's been in and out most of the night."

Peter nodded. "She's been through a lot."

Jess gazed down at her friend. "Yeah, she has."

Peter cleared his throat. "Jess, about last night, I'm sorry if what I said came out wrong. I was distraught. All I could think was that something could have happened to you. I'm sorry."

She smiled sadly. "I'm sorry, too."

He walked over and kissed her gently.

She leaned into her husband. "So, any news about what happens next?"

"Well, like you said, the case against Daniel is over. Without a defendant, there is no case. Which also means this nightmare is finally over."

"No," came a whisper from the bed. "It's not. It's not even close to being over."

Peter looked over at Victoria. "What do you mean?"

Before Victoria could answer, the doctor walked in. "Hello, everyone. I'm afraid I'll have to ask you to leave so that I can examine the patient."

Jess turned towards Victoria again. She wanted to ask Victoria what she meant, but with the doctor there, she knew that she wouldn't get the answers right then.

****

Two days later, Victoria was sitting up in bed watching television. Jess studied her friend from the doorway. The swelling in her face was beginning to subside. The color of her bruises were worse, but she knew they would fade in time.

"Hi, Victoria," Jess said, smiling as she handed Victoria a coffee. "You're starting to look better. How are you feeling?"

Victoria turned off the television and turned her head towards Jess. She tried to smile as she took the coffee. "I feel like I've been run over by a Mack truck."

She took a sip and sighed. "Oh my, this is so good. I think I'll survive now."

Jess sat down in the chair next to the bed and faced Victoria. "I'm sorry you went through that. At least now you don't have to be afraid anymore."

"I wasn't afraid of Daniel's wrath," Victoria said quietly. "It's everyone else that I'm worried about."

"What do you mean?" asked Jess.

"Never mind," Victoria replied. She took a sip of her coffee and closed her eyes.

"Tell me, Victoria. Aren't you tired of all these secrets?"

"I'm not keeping secrets, just stating the facts. Daniel's dead, and that's going to piss off a lot of people. He was a major supplier and had a booming operation, not to mention everyone in town that depended on him to keep them afloat."

Jess thought about what Victoria was telling her. "How did he help people around here? I mean, I know he funded the park, but how did that impact business?"

"Oh Jess, you have so much to learn. If people in this town couldn't get a loan for their business, they'd go to Daniel. If their business was in financial trouble, Daniel would help them out. In exchange, everyone around here laundered his money. Each business received a payout in exchange for their cooperation. There are people higher up that are going to expect continued cooperation. They are also going to get their revenge on whoever killed Daniel."

"Well, that wasn't you," Jess said carefully, "It was David."

"Yeah, things aren't going to go well for David, but it was because of me that David shot him in the first place. It's because of you that we're in this mess to begin with. If you were in the mafia, who would you hold responsible?

They're not going to just come after David. They are going to make examples of us. They're going to come after us, too. I told you to leave me alone. I told you to mind your own business. I told you."

Jess stood up. "Wait a minute, you told me to mind my own business, but your husband was beating you so badly you could have died. Instead of blaming me, maybe you should be thanking me. As for all of these businesses and Daniel, we'll figure it out. Surely, they couldn't have been happy with what was going on. We can leave, Victoria. We can go into witness protection. We can move. We don't have to live in fear. We don't have to live here."

Victoria looked at her incredulously. She raised her voice. "Says who? You? My whole life is here. All I have is The Blooming Boutique. I've sacrificed everything for that place. Jess, stay the hell away from me, and you can start by getting out of my room."

Jess felt like she had just been slapped. In the back of her mind, she could hear a voice saying *you can't help those who don't want to be helped.* She shook her head sadly, and without saying a word, she picked up her jacket and walked out of the room.

Stepping outside the hospital, she started walking towards her car then changed her mind, turned around, and walked east towards the cafe around the corner. While walking, she thought about her conversation with Victoria. She believed Victoria when she said they were still in danger. There had to be a way to end this nightmare. Maybe if she could figure out who the previous owners of her house were, she could find out who else was in Daniel's drug ring. That was the missing piece. She was certain of it.

Jess walked into the cafe and ordered a coffee. She thought about Victoria. How could she just throw away their friendship? How could Victoria want to stay here? Hopefully, in time, Victoria will come to her senses. She finished her coffee and walked back out in the cool, crisp air. She sank down into her jacket trying to stay warm and walked towards her car.

She climbed into her car and called George.

"Hi Jess," George answered on the third ring. "I was just thinking about you. How are you?"

Jess frowned. "I'm doing much better, thanks. I'm actually calling you about Daniel's wife, Victoria."

"What's happened?"

Jess told George about what had happened at Daniel's house, ending with David shooting Daniel.

The other end of the line was quiet for a minute, then George asked, "How is Victoria?"

Jess's heart plunged at the sound of Victoria's name. "Well, she blames me for this whole thing. Apparently, I am the reason that Daniel is dead. It doesn't matter that I probably saved her life, she seems to think otherwise."

"In a way, she's right," George replied. "With every action, there's a reaction. A lot of people were involved in Daniel's dealings, some of them just as powerful. They will want answers."

Jess exhaled loudly. "That's what she thinks."

"With that said, give her some time," George said. "She's been through a lot. She's a victim, Jess. Probably as much a victim as you are."

"I guess," Jess replied. "Anyway, I was calling to see if you found out anything about the Wellingtons?"

George sighed. "Not really. With hardly any information to go on, I feel like they probably met their demise when they figured out what Daniel was doing. I don't have proof yet, but that's the only thing that makes sense in all this. I'll keep looking, and keep you posted. Say, we found a flash drive with code names and money amounts. We're thinking it might be his contacts. We're trying to decipher it now. Maybe it might point us in the right direction."

"I hope so. I never heard Daniel say his employees' names. I'm fairly sure that the man with the scar down his face worked very closely with Daniel."

"Would you be able to pick him out if you saw a picture of him, or saw him in a lineup?"

Jess shivered. "Yes, he gives me the creeps. I could easily identify him. He has a long scar down his left cheek, dark hair, and dark soulless eyes. He was always at the drop-offs at Daniel's, and I'm pretty sure he was in the truck that tried to run me off the road last month."

George was quiet for a minute and then replied, "Let me get ahold of my friend in the department and see if we can connect him to Daniel and bring him in. Maybe we can scare him into giving us information about the Wellingtons."

Jess felt relieved hearing this. "Thanks, George."

****

The next week, Jess was doing her physical therapy exercises when her phone rang.

"Hi, George. This is a surprise."

"I've got someone at the precinct that can see you and have you go through some pictures. Are you free this afternoon?"

"I am. Where is the precinct located?"

"You'll have to drive to Albany. The guy you'll meet with is Max. He's put together some albums with men who have a scar on their cheek."

"I'll be there."

Jess changed her clothes and grabbed her keys. She called Sampson, and he came, wagging his tail. They both walked out the door and climbed into the rental car.

As she drove past Daniel's house, she gripped the steering wheel tightly. She knew Victoria was there, and wondered how she was doing, but she wasn't going to stop. If Victoria wanted her to stay away, then that's what she'd do.

She kept driving until she reached Albany. Parking the car, she turned to Sampson. Stroking his head she said, "Be good, boy. I won't be long." The cooler temperatures ensured that he would be comfortable while she was gone. Closing the door behind her, she walked into the precinct and asked for Max.

The receptionist led her to a desk where a short, stocky man was sitting in front of a computer. On the side of his desk were three photo albums.

Nervously, she sat down.

"Mrs. Stanton, thanks for coming in. I've assembled some photo albums for you. Take your time when you go through them, and if you see any pictures that look familiar to you, take them out and I'll check into them."

She nodded as he handed her the first album. She opened the cover and slowly studied each man. Each man had a scar on his left cheek. Some had dark hair, some blond hair, some no hair at all. They were all sizes and shapes. She studied the eyes. She knew she wouldn't forget those eyes. They made her blood curl.

By the third album, Jess was starting to get discouraged. All the pictures were starting to blend together until she reached a page with those eyes staring back at her. Her hands were shaking when she took his picture out of the album.

"Here you go," she said as she handed the picture to Max.

"Thanks. Are there anymore that you found?"

She shook her head. "No, he's the one. I don't need any others. I know it's him."

He looked at the picture again. "We'll follow up with this. Thanks for your help."

Jess stood up and took one last look at the picture lying on his desk. She had no doubt that he was Daniel's goon.

She left the precinct hoping this could lead to the Wellingtons. She hoped this wouldn't open up another can of worms but would instead lead to a resolution.

****

Jess was cleaning out the drawers in the kitchen, hoping she'd come across another clue from the Wellingtons-- if it was in fact even a clue to begin with. There had to be more.

She pulled out the last drawer and looked underneath it. There was a space between the drawer and the floor. Lying there was a stack of papers stapled together. She carefully pulled them out.

It was the loan paperwork for Peter's law office and the house. The loan didn't come from a bank that Peter's old firm in the city used. The name of the person supplying the loan was Daniel Easton.

Jess sat on the floor, staring at the papers. Why would Daniel be giving Peter the loan for the law office and the house? Why would Peter lie about it? Has Peter worked for Daniel all along? She put the papers underneath the drawer. Jess was livid. How could she have been so naïve? She would wait and confront Peter about it on her own terms. At the moment she didn't think she could stand the sight of him.

Chapter 21

That night, Peter came home once again looking disheveled. His tie was loosened, his hair was sticking up, and he appeared to have spilled coffee on the front of his shirt. Exhaustion was written all over his face.

"Tough day?" Jess asked, trying to keep her anger at bay. *Soon,* she promised herself. *Once I find out if Peter was working for Daniel.*

"You could say that!" Peter replied angrily. "Since Daniel's been gone, I'm a pariah in this town. No one wants anything to do with me."

"Honey, I'm sure that's not true. It's a small town. We just need for things to calm down." Jess felt guilty that Peter was going through this. He didn't ask for this, but she was relieved that Daniel was gone.

Peter grabbed her by the arms. "It is true, and you're right, it is a small town. You have managed to single-handedly ruin my business and my reputation."

Jess tried to wrench her arms away, but he held her fast. "Peter, you're hurting me. Let me go… you're hurting me!"

"Hurting you? Why couldn't you just mind your own business? You kept asking about Daniel, you kept asking about this house. No one cared but you. Why couldn't you just leave things alone? You want to know why we moved here? The firm sent me. I didn't tell you because it's none of your business! We could have made this work, but you just couldn't let things go. There's your answer. That was the big secret. Happy now?"

"Happy? Hell no I'm not happy, Peter. I'm far from happy. I found the papers."

"What papers," Peter retorted.

"The papers showing that Daniel was the one behind the loan for the house and office. I want to know. Were you working for him?"

He scoffed. "Of course I was. You knew that. I was his lawyer!"

Jess was livid. "You know what I mean, Peter. Are you part of Daniel's organization?"

He glared at her, then released her. "I'm not going to answer such an absurd question. You've really sunk to a new low, Jess."

He grabbed a beer from the refrigerator and walked upstairs. Jess picked up a glass from the table and threw it against the wall. "You son of a bitch," she yelled.

A few minutes later, he stomped back down, carrying a duffel bag and his briefcase.

"What do you think you're doing?" Jess asked, bewildered.

"I'm staying at a motel, if they'll even rent me a room for the night. I need some space to think."

"Peter--"

"Jess, stop," Peter interrupted. He continued walking out the door and headed towards his truck.

"Shit!" he yelled.

Jess followed him.

As she got closer to the truck, she noticed that all the tires had been slashed on both vehicles.

Peter looked at Jess. "Still don't believe me?" he asked sarcastically.

He pulled out his phone and dialed the police station.

He stared at Jess with malevolence as he spoke to someone at the station. Once he hung up the phone, he muttered, "David will be out to make a report."

Jess sighed. "I'm sorry, Peter. I didn't know."

Peter glared at her. She had never seen him so angry. "Yes," he yelled. "You didn't know… you didn't NEED to know. It was NONE of your business, but you MADE it your business. YOU caused this. YOU… YOU, YOU!"

David pulled into the driveway just as it started to rain. Putting on his hat, he stepped out of his car. He walked over and inspected the vehicles. "Someone slashed the tires. There's no doubt about that one. Every once in a while, we get some kids doing this as a dare."

Pulling out a camera, he began taking pictures of each tire. The rain began to fall harder, and David looked at the black storm clouds in the sky. "Come down to the station in the morning, and we'll finish filling out a report."

Jess smiled at David. "Do you want to come in for a cup of coffee?"

"No, I've got to get back."

Jess nodded; his message received. There would be no easy chats anytime soon.

Once he left, Jess and Peter walked back inside. He stomped back upstairs towards his office and slammed the door.

Jess ambled into the kitchen and put some water on to boil for tea. She looked outside, watching the rain and wondering, not for the first time, how their house went from a place where they lived to a place of threats and danger. She thought back to the first time she had a flat tire, and wondered if there was a connection, if Daniel and his goons were behind it. It wasn't the first time she had wondered this, but now she was positive they were.

Slipping on a jacket, she stepped outside. Even though Peter was in his office, he still didn't feel far enough away from her. She rubbed her arms where he had grabbed her earlier.

Glancing towards Victoria's house, she noticed the black car parked in the front. It worried her, but she was determined not to interfere in Victoria's life any longer. *You can't help people who didn't want to be helped*, she reminded herself. There was a clap of thunder and a strike of lightning.

Turning around, she ambled back inside as the tea kettle began to whistle. She turned off the stove just as the lights went out.

"Great," she muttered. It wasn't the first time they'd lost electricity.

Peter stomped downstairs, strode past Jess without saying a word, and opened the circuit breaker box.

"It doesn't look like it's a circuit. We must have lost electricity again," Peter muttered.

Jess shivered and rubbed her arms. "It seems like a big coincidence, don't you think?"

Peter rolled his eyes. "Well, I think we can safely say that it's not Daniel."

Jess put her hands on her hips and glared at him. "If you'd believed me earlier, maybe it wouldn't have come to this!"

He turned on her. "Don't you blame this on me. This is all on you, Jess. So we have slashed tires. David said it was probably some kids on a dare. Jesus, when are you going to stop!"

"Victoria told us there would be retaliation once Daniel was dead. Are you that dense?"

"No, Jess, I'm not dense, sweetheart. I'm done. I'm done with interfering where you're not wanted. I'm done with listening to your theories. You created this, now you live with it."

An animal-like scream came from outside. Sampson stood up and barked frantically. Without thinking, Jess ran to the door and followed Sampson outside. Through the deluge of rain, she could see Victoria being chased by the man with the scar, the man who had threatened Jess on the road. He grabbed Victoria by the arm, and they both fell to the ground.

"Where's the money, bitch? You're his wife-- I know you have it-- where is it?" he yelled.

"I don't know!" Victoria screamed, hitting him weakly.

Jess picked up a branch and ran towards them. "Let her go!" she yelled.

Before Jess could get to them, Sampson attacked the man by sinking his teeth into his leg. The man let go of Victoria and turned on the dog. Victoria jumped up and sprinted towards Jess, and both women ran to the house.

"Peter, call David! Call 9-1-1. Hurry!" Jess screamed.

Peter was still standing in the doorway when she and Victoria ran into the house. Jess saw him shake his head as they ran past. "You two bitches have single-handedly ruined everything I've worked for, and now you want my help. Unbelievable. You reap what you sow."

Jess locked the door, then ran through the house to lock the back door.

Victoria was bleeding from a cut on the side of her head. With a shaky hand, she wiped some of the blood away, which just made it look worse. A yelp came from outside as the man kicked at Sampson.

"Sampson!" Jess yelled, and the dog came running to the kitchen door. She quickly let him in and locked the door. Next, a rock sailed through a window in the living room.

"Victoria, hide," Jess ordered. She grabbed a butcher knife and walked towards the living room as Victoria grabbed another knife and went to hide in the pantry.

With a shaking hand, Jess pulled out her phone and dialed 9-1-1. She really hoped it wouldn't be David, but David had helped her out before when he shot Daniel, so maybe he'd help again.

****

Peter shook his head. "Unbelievable," he muttered again. He walked upstairs, and once again he grabbed his duffel bag. He was done with this charade. Jess never listened to him. She never followed his advice. If she wanted to go after this guy halfcocked, then let her.

He opened the window and crawled out onto the roof. He looked down. It wasn't too far of a jump. He threw his bag down, and then slid off the roof.

When Peter hit the ground, his ankle twisted. "Shit!" he cried out as a searing pain ran up his leg. He knew his ankle was broken.

He could hear Jess yelling inside the house. "You bastard!" Sampson was still growling in the background.

Peter stood up and dragged himself around to the side of the house. Sampson came running behind him, barking wildly. How the dog managed to get out of the house, he didn't know.

The man with the scar stopped trying to climb in through the broken window and charged towards the side of the house at Peter instead.

Peter, trying to balance his weight on one foot, held up both hands in surrender. "Whoa, wait a minute," Peter yelled. "I'm on your side. I don't care what you do with the girls."

The man pointed a gun at Peter. "I don't believe you."

"C'mon, man," Peter said licking his lips nervously. "I can keep a secret. I was defending Daniel. I'm on your side, I swear."

"You were defending Daniel because Daniel told you too. It wasn't your choice. You're lying!" the man shouted.

"No, stop, I swear!" Peter begged, sagging down onto the muddy ground.

****

Jess heard Peter's voice outside. Her heart sank. They may have been fighting but she didn't want him to die. Knife in hand she ran towards their voices. "Stay away from him!" she ordered.

The man with the scar turned and grabbed Jess's arm before she could make contact. He twisted her arm behind her back, and she dropped the knife. "Stop!" she screamed out in pain. Shoving Jess towards Peter, he then bent down and picked up the knife. Pointing it in Jess's direction, he glared at her. "You wouldn't be so concerned if you knew that your man here was trying to sell you out. Claims he was on Daniel's side the whole time."

Jess looked at Peter. She saw the cold steel of his eyes and the square set of his jaw in defiance. She shook her head. The man was right.

As much as she wanted to kill Peter right now, she didn't want to give the other man the privilege.

"Where's Victoria? Get her out here too," ordered the man.

"Victoria!" Jess yelled, but there was no reply. Victoria didn't walk out the door.

Jess thought fast. "Let me go talk to her. I can get her to come out, and we can all talk about this."

She tried to keep her face blank as she saw Victoria come from the front of the house and creep up behind the man, holding a big rock, ready to smash it onto his head.

Jess prayed Peter would keep his mouth shut as she continued to distract the man.

"Was it you who killed the Wellingtons?" she accused. "Is that why no one knows where they are?"

Just as Victoria raised the rock, a voice yelled, "Drop the rock, Victoria!" Victoria, startled, did as she was told.

David stepped out of the tree line with his gun pointed.

The man smiled menacingly and said, "Great timing. Seems like we've got a problem with these three."

David's expression was grim as he looked at the three victims huddled together. "I see that," he replied calmly.

"Should we get rid of them like we did the others?"

Jess couldn't help herself. "Like the Wellingtons? Is that who you're talking about?"

"Jesus Christ, Jess, just let it go!" Peter yelled at her.

The man took the bait. "What is it with you nosy people? Can't you just mind your own business? You people just have to always be poking around." He waved the gun around before pointing it at Jess.

"On the ground, everyone, on the ground," yelled a voice in the darkness.

The man with the scar looked at David. "What the hell is going on?"

"I don't know, Bobby," David muttered.

"Police! You're surrounded! Everyone, on the ground! NOW! Do it NOW!"

Men dressed in black with lights mounted on their guns started coming towards them from all directions. They were surrounded.

David and Bobby dropped their guns and put their hands in the air. In a flurry, men from the SWAT team surrounded them and led David and Bobby away in handcuffs. Once the women were no longer deemed a threat, they were able to stand up.

An ambulance pulled up and Victoria, Jess, and Peter were directed to it to be checked out. Peter, with an arm slung around a paramedic, limped towards the ambulance.

Jess looked at him. "What happened to your ankle?"

"I tried to distract him by running outside, and I rolled my ankle."

Jess shook her head. "Give it up, Peter. You're a coward. You always have been. We moved up here because you screwed up when we lived in the city. You think I don't know what you're up to? I looked into it when you were gung-ho on moving here. I'm not stupid. I never was but I am disappointed that you couldn't be truthful with me."

She walked off with her head held high, towards Victoria, who was giving a statement.

"Mrs. Stanton?"

She stopped and turned her head and saw a green-eyed man with a black knit hat pulled over his head looking at her. "Yes," she replied.

He walked towards her and showed her his badge. "I'm Inspector Wyatt Miller from the NY State Police. I'm in charge of this case and I have a few questions for you. Would you mind coming with me?"

Jess followed him to his surveillance van. As the adrenaline drained away, she began shivering.

Inspector Miller turned up the heat in the van. "Are you alright? Did you get checked out?"

She shrugged. "I'm alright." In reality, her heart was beating rapidly in her chest. She wondered if she was going to have a heart attack. She fought to control her breathing. "Victoria's pretty banged up, though."

Wyatt handed her a bottle of water. "Can you tell me what happened here?" He pulled out a notebook.

Jess recounted the events of the night. She walked him through everything: the slashed tires, the electricity going out, and ending with the standoff.

Wyatt looked at her intently. "I've got to ask, and you're probably not going to like it, but was your husband working for Mr. Easton?"

She looked up at him and shook her head. "No… yes…" She shrugged. "I don't know. I didn't think so, but I found some paperwork he had hidden away saying Daniel was the one who loaned us the money for the law office and the house. I feel like I don't know anything, anymore."

Wyatt looked up from writing and said, "I noticed cameras outside of your house. Did they record the events that happened tonight?"

Jess looked at him in surprise. "I never thought of that. Yes, they work. It should all be on the cameras."

Wyatt wrote down her statement and then cleared his throat. "We have a friend in common."

"Oh, yeah? Who?" Jess asked suspiciously.

"George Myers," Wyatt replied.

"George? How do you know George?"

"He's my grandfather."

Recognition was starting to dawn on her. "You're his contact."

He smiled wryly. "Yes, I'm his contact." Wyatt studied her. "I've been working on this case night and day since he told me about it. Once Easton met his demise, I knew it was only a matter of time before there would be a retaliation. We set up a surveillance team to keep an eye on Victoria, and your house just happened to be in the general vicinity. So, let me ask you, was your husband involved in the retaliation towards Mrs. Easton?"

Jess scoffed. "Peter is nothing but a coward. Trust me, he doesn't have balls big enough to run with the big boys. He was running away. I don't think he wanted to get caught in the crossfire. And please stop referring to him as my husband. He won't be in the near future."

Wyatt looked like he was trying not to smile at her statement. "Yes, Ma'am."

Before he could ask another question, Jess asked one of her own. "If you work so closely with George, then you must know that we're trying to find out about what happened to the Wellingtons. They were the people who previously owned my house."

Wyatt nodded. "George has discussed it with me, and we have a few theories that we're looking into."

The door to the van opened up. "Sir, we're ready to take the suspects back to the precinct for questioning."

Wyatt nodded at the agent. "I'll be right behind you. Did you make sure that you read them their rights? I don't want anything jeopardizing this case."

"Yes, sir," the agent responded as he shut the door.

Wyatt looked at Jess once more. "Don't leave town in case we have any more questions. I also suggest that you find somewhere else to stay for the night. It might be safer."

Jess agreed and let herself out of the van. The ambulance was leaving, with Peter presumably inside it. She was surprised to see Victoria walking towards her.

"Why aren't you leaving in the ambulance?" Jess asked.

Victoria shook her head. "I've been worse off than this. It's just superficial. I'll be alright." She motioned towards the driveway. "They took Peter off to the hospital. Do you need a ride?"

Jess rolled her eyes. "I think I'll let Peter sort this one out on his own. I'm done being his doormat. Did they get your statement?"

"Yes, hopefully this will be the end of it." Although they both knew that it wasn't.

After the ambulance left, the federal agents followed. It was quieter now. The two houses looked eerily still. Wyatt walked over to Jess and Victoria.

"Would you ladies like a ride somewhere? Technically, this place is a crime scene now."

Jess looked at Victoria and shrugged. "Do you have a suggestion of where?"

"There's a bed and breakfast a few miles away," Victoria said. She yawned. "Do you want to stay there?"

Jess ran her hands up and down her arms. "Sure, that would be great."

"Can I drive my car, or is that part of the crime scene?" Victoria asked Wyatt.

Wyatt shrugged. "No, you're free to drive your car."

"Great. Jess, you want a ride?"

"Sure," Jess replied. Turning to Wyatt she said, "Thank you for all of your help, Wyatt."

Victoria raised her eyebrow at Jess. "Wyatt?" she mouthed.

Jess shook her head and smiled slowly. "Later," she mouthed as they started walking towards the car.

They were exhausted as they got in the car. It was over now. At least, they hoped so.

Chapter 22

Inspector Wyatt Miller sat across from David in the interrogation room. David hung his head not wanting to look at anyone. He knew he had been caught. He glanced at the two-way mirrors, knowing there were others watching him. He couldn't bargain with Inspector Miller, not while there were other witnesses.

"I want my lawyer," David hissed. "I won't say another word until my lawyer is present."

Inspector Miller smiled. "David, you know the drill. We can make a deal and make this go away. Think about it."

"That's a lie," David growled.

The Inspector stopped smiling. He leaned over and said, "Do you want this whole thing to blow up in your face? You know how things work. I have the power to make this whole nightmare go away."

"I don't believe you," David retorted. "I'm not that stupid."

Inspector Miller shrugged. "Never mind. Suit yourself. You know how much convicts love bad cops." He pushed back his chair and walked out the door, slamming it behind him.

****

Inspector Miller strode across the hall and walked into the room where Bobby was sitting. He pulled out a chair and sat down across from him. Opening a folder that he had brought in with him, he reached into his pocket and took out a pack of cigarettes. With the flick of the lighter, he lit one and handed it to Bobby.

"Thanks," Bobby said as he took it and inhaled deeply. The Inspector nodded and started reading the top page.

"Impressive rap sheet, Bobby. I see you've done some time and have been out for about a year. You, David, and Daniel had quite the racket going on."

"You don't know anything," Bobby barked. "Where's my lawyer?"

"It's a funny thing about lawyers," Inspector Miller said confidently. "David was asking for one, too. When his lawyer arrived, he started singing like a bird."

Bobby laughed. "He doesn't have anything to sing about. He's a dirty cop. He always has been."

"That could be," said Inspector Miller nonchalantly, "But he seemed to have a lot to say about you."

Bobby stopped laughing and slammed his fist on the table. "You're lying."

"Am I?" The two men stared at one another. The Inspector continued on. "What do you know about the Wellingtons?"

"Who?" Bobby took a drag off his cigarette. "Is that the nosy woman who was always in Daniel's business?"

Inspector Miller shook his head. "No, it's not. This would be the previous owners of the house that is now owned by the so-called nosy neighbor. Seems they just disappeared into thin air. What happened to them?"

"No idea." Bobby shrugged noncommittally. "I'm not trying to tell you how to do your job, but aren't you supposed to be asking me about what happened tonight?"

The Inspector returned the paper to the folder and stood up. "I could, but you'd just lawyer up. I'll leave that to the federal agents. We've been watching you for a while, now. We've got what we need. Now, if you want to talk about the Wellingtons, maybe we could make a deal."

"Never heard of them."

Inspector Miller waited a bit before shrugging and saying, "That's too bad. David said you knew all about the Wellingtons, insinuating, in fact, that you were the one who killed them."

"What? That's bullshit. I ain't killed nobody."

"I figured you'd try to deny it. Well, it doesn't matter. It's late, and you'll be arraigned in the morning."

Bobby stood up. "What am I being charged for?"

“Destroying property, breaking and entering, assault, murder--”

Bobby stood and slammed his fist down on the table once again. Two officers came in and pushed him back down in his chair. “I’m telling you, I didn’t murder anyone.”

The Inspector took out another cigarette and lit it. He inhaled, then exhaled. The smoke billowed up towards the ceiling. “The way I see it,” Inspector Miller said, “It’s not me you have to convince, but a jury of your peers. Now, who do you think they’re going to believe? You, or our illustrious sheriff?”

Two officers led Bobby out of the room. “I’m telling you, I didn’t do it!” yelled Bobby.

Inspector Miller took a tissue out of the box and bent over to retrieve the cigarette butt Bobby had left smashed on the floor. The DNA would be useful.

****

Inspector Miller walked back into the room where David was sitting. “Seems like your friend, Bobby, had a lot to say. He sends his regards, by the way.”

David didn’t respond. “How long do you intend to keep me cooped up? I’ve got work to do.”

"I think that'll have to wait, Sheriff. From what I see, you look just as guilty as your friend Bobby."

David huffed. "A lot you know. I was undercover. I had it under control until you guys came barreling in. I can prove it with my reports."

The Inspector shook his head. "Save it for your lawyer."

"Speaking of lawyer, I want to call mine."

"Who are you going to call? I'll get the number for you."

"No need," said David. "He's local, and I've got his number. The name is Peter Stanton."

Inspector Miller shook his head and laughed. "You think the person who's a victim and is currently in the hospital is going to defend you? You must be delusional."

David stared at him stone-faced. "I'm entitled to my phone call."

The Inspector shrugged and put his hands up in mock surrender. "Alright, alright. Make your phone call. I'll leave you to it. See you in the morning when we go before the judge."

David called Peter's phone.

"Peter Stanton."

David leaned against the wall of the pay phone. "Peter, David here. I'm in need of your services. How soon can you get down to the station?"

Peter was silent for a minute before replying. "I don't think that's going to be possible."

"Are you still in the hospital?" David asked.

"No, but I'm still in a lot of pain. David, it's not a good idea for me to represent you. I'm a victim in this case. I'll be testifying against you."

The guard signaled to David that his time was almost up. David nodded. "I don't think that'll happen. We're connected, you and me. We've been seen together at Daniel's parties and talking around town. You were defending Daniel before his untimely death."

"That's ridiculous," Peter retorted. "Daniel was threatening my wife's life. I didn't have a choice."

David hissed into the phone, "You don't have a choice now, either. Daniel told me all about your screw-ups in the city, and how he got you the house next door. You were working with him just like every one of us were. You're not innocent. Don't pretend to be."

He hung up the phone and looked at the guard. He was being kept in a special holding cell separate from the other inmates, at least for the time being. Until he was either found guilty or allowed to resume his life.

****

As David was being led into the conference room, he saw Peter drumming his fingers impatiently on the table. He must have been waiting for a while.

David grinned. "Well, there's my lawyer. I'm glad you came around to my way of thinking."

Peter scowled as he repositioned his crutches against the wall. He opened up a folder and began reading through the charges.

Inspector Miller came walking into the room. He was dressed in a dark suit with his hair slicked back. He sat down across from Peter and motioned for David to sit down.

"What are you doing here?" David demanded. "I didn't ask for anyone except for my lawyer."

Inspector Miller held out a hand to Peter. "I don't believe we've officially met. I was there the night we arrested Mr. Harris and Mr. Smith. You were already in the ambulance by the time I was finished." He motioned to Peter's leg. "How is your leg doing?"

Peter shook his hand then motioned towards his cast. "It's healing."

"We're here for my arraignment, not a meet and greet," David growled. "Now, if you'll excuse us, we've got some things to take care of."

The Inspector stood up and walked to the door. He turned the lock, then strode back to the table and sat back down.

"Chad and Claudia Wellington," Inspector Miller said as he pulled two pictures out of his folder and set them in front David.

"What?" David asked, confused. "What does this have to do with my arraignment? Get the hell out of here," he barked.

Peter looked at the pictures. "Why are you asking about the Wellingtons?"

Inspector Miller pushed the pictures a little closer to David. "I'm proposing a deal. You give me information about what happened to the Wellingtons, and maybe we can make all of this go away."

David laughed. "Do I look stupid to you? I'm a cop, too. Cops can't make deals, that's for the prosecution to handle." He pointed to Peter. "I have a lawyer who can handle my case. I don't need you, and I had nothing to do with what happened to the Wellingtons."

The Inspector zeroed in. "What makes you think something *happened* to the Wellingtons?"

David glared at him. "Why would you be asking me about them if nothing happened?"

Tapping his watch he said, "We're running out of time, here. It's your decision. Tell me what you know. I know they're dead."

David shrugged. "I don't know anything. Now, if you have no other questions, I'd like to meet with my lawyer."

Inspector Miller stretched over and turned off the recorder. He also motioned for the cameras to be turned off."

Peter stood up. "You can't do this. I'll get him off if you lay a hand on him."

The Inspector stood up and winked at the two-way mirror, signaling for them to come in. A deputy walked in and dragged Peter out of the room.

"You can't do this!" Peter yelled as the metal door slammed behind him.

The Inspector grabbed David by the shirt and threw him up against the concrete wall. Holding him there, he whispered, "Listen, you son of a bitch, I'm trying to help you. You're a bad cop, and you know what they do to bad cops in prison. I hate bad cops, and I usually don't help the bad guy, but I want the Wellingtons, and I don't give a shit about what deal you had with Daniel. I'm having DNA tested right now to prove Bobby killed the Wellingtons. I just need you to cooperate. Tell me what happened and where they are, and I will guarantee your freedom. This is a deal between you and me, not our lawyers, not the prosecution, not the law. Take it or leave it."

David pushed himself free and looked back at the two-way mirrors. "How do I know no one is watching me right now? How do I know you're telling the truth?"

"You don't, but what other choice do you have?"

David pulled out the chair and sat down. Inspector Miller sat down across from him and waited for David's decision.

"Alright, I swear I had nothing to do with them, but yes, they are dead. They got too nosy about Daniel, and he made sure they wouldn't talk."

"Who killed them?"

David shook his head. "I can't tell you that. If I do, I'm a dead man."

The Inspector crossed his arms. "If you go to jail, you're a dead man. If you tell me, you can disappear. Retire and move anywhere in the world. Everyone already knows you shot Daniel; I'm giving you a way out. Take it."

David thought about what he said. He was right. If David went to jail, he would be as good as dead.

Warily, he asked, "What do you want to know?"

"Did Smith kill them, and where are they buried?"

"They're buried somewhere up on Rusk Mountain."

Inspector Miller quickly wrote the information down. "Who killed them?"

David hesitated. He knew if he said anything more there would be no going back.

"David, I'm guaranteeing your freedom."

"Bobby. Bobby shot them both."

The Inspector leaned closer. "Tell me what happened."

David looked down, defeated. "Bobby broke into the house. He was just going to scare them off, at first. He didn't want anyone asking questions about their disappearance if he were to kill them. He went after Chad first. Chad fought back. Then Claudia came in. She saw Chad laying on the floor and lost it. She grabbed a knife and went after Bobby. That's how he got that scar on his face. Bobby shot her. He didn't have a choice. That's the only way he could get her off him. He didn't want any witnesses, so he shot Chad, too." He called me to help clean up the mess and get rid of the bodies."

Inspector Miller leaned back in his chair, his face not revealing anything that he was thinking. "Do you remember where the bodies are buried?"

David ran a hand down his face. "Yeah, I can get you there."

"Great, I'll get a crew together, and you can lead us to them."

"Wait," said David, "What should I tell Peter?"

"You can say you decided to cooperate, fire him, I don't really care. Just have him out of the way by the time we pick you up to go to Rusk Mountain."

Chapter 23

Peter reentered the room. “David, don’t say anything. I’ll get you off. These guys just screwed up.”

“You’re fired,” David announced.

“What? You got attacked in the interrogation room and now you’re firing me? I don’t think so. We can fight this. We won’t even go to trial when I’m done with them. Do you have any marks we can document?”

David shook his head. “You’re fired. You can go, Peter.”

Peter looked bewildered. “Are you sure you’re not being coerced? Think about what you’re saying. I can get you off. I can pretty much guarantee it.”

David stared at him, unwavering. “Please leave, and don’t come back.”

Peter threw his hands in the air. “You don’t know what you’re doing.” He shrugged but did as he was told.

****

David sat on the thin mattress of his bunk, waiting for Inspector Miller to get the crew together. The steel bars felt like they were closing in on him. He thought about the deal they had struck. It was a gamble, that was for sure. Was he really going to get through this alive? What if he showed them where the Wellingtons were buried, and then they killed him? How did he know that The Inspector wasn't in Daniel's pockets, too? If Inspector Miller was a law-abiding cop, then what would possess him to break the law and help?

He had so many questions, and unfortunately, no answers. This was his only shot at freedom. His only shot at staying alive. He'd take it. He really didn't have any other choice.

David stretched out and bunched up the thin piece of foam that was supposed to be a pillow. He knew it would be a while before Inspector Miller could put a team together.

He thought back to the night the Wellingtons were killed. He didn't even know why Bobby had called him to help, and every day since, he had regretted helping him. David had entered the front door into the living room and seen Chad's lifeless body lying in a pool of blood on the floor. It must have been some fight, because there was blood on the furniture, walls, and floor. Lamps and knickknacks littered the floor.

Bobby had turned and looked at him. Blood was oozing from a cut down his cheek. Claudia's body lay in an awkward position on the floor. A gunshot had gone through her chest. Her eyes, still open, were empty and devoid of life.

"Jesus," David had muttered. "What the hell happened?"

"They fought instead of just cowering and crying in a corner," Bobby said, walking into the kitchen and wetting a towel to put on his cheek. "Daniel's going to be pissed. We've got to get this cleaned up."

The two men loaded the bodies into the back of a pickup truck and covered them with a tarp. They climbed in the front of the cab. David called Daniel and told him what had happened. There was no way in hell he'd be keeping this secret. He hung up the phone and looked back at Bobby. "Daniel is going to send a crew out to clean this mess up. He wants us to make sure we get rid of them in a place where they'll never be found."

Bobby started up the truck, and they pulled out of the driveway and headed west towards Rusk Mountain. They rode in silence. David began replaying the night's events in his head and he was sure Bobby was, too. An hour later, Bobby parked at the mouth of the hiking trail. They grabbed Claudia first. Bobby slung her petite frame over his shoulder as David grabbed the two shovels. They walked in silence for about a quarter of a mile, then Bobby veered off the trail and into the woods. He stumbled over tree roots and dead branches laying on the ground, but quickly found his footing again. A light rain began to make the ground slippery. The two men stopped and rested. "

About another third of a mile should do it," Bobby said. "It'll be far enough from the main trail that nobody will know they're there."

David nodded in agreement. The blood that was still trailing from Bobby's face made him look like the grotesque monster that he was.

The rain began to fall harder and began to wash the blood trail away. The dead weight of the body was beginning to take its toll. They each grabbed a foot and dragged Claudia the rest of the way. Once they were finished with Claudia, they walked back to the truck and got Chad. He was heavier, and the rain was making the ground slick. They had no other choice but to drag Chad. They put his body on a tarp and each man took a corner. They dragged his body to where Claudia lay.

When they reached their destination, they picked up their shovels and began to dig in the rocky soil. At least the rain helped to soften the dirt somewhat. It took hours before the two victims were buried deep enough to keep away the wildlife. At least, the two men hoped so. The sun was beginning to rise in the east.

****

The sound of a metal door opening roused David from his unpleasant reminiscing.

The Inspector walked into the room and looked at David. "I've lined up a team… let's go." He pulled out a pair of handcuffs. "These are for you, just in case you decide to make a break for it." He locked the handcuffs in place, and led David from the cell.

The other prisoners hurled catcalls, insults, and threats at David as he was led down the corridor between the cells. David cringed, thinking he might have to live with these people. He prayed the deal he made would ensure his freedom.

David squinted in the bright sunlight as his gaze fell on the convoy of law enforcement that would follow in his wake. He was led to the back of an unmarked car. The Inspector walked around to the trunk of the car and retrieved his sidearm. David didn't see one marked police car. He assumed this was to not draw attention to the real purpose of his trip. Maybe Inspector Miller was on the up-and-up and he could get out of this unscathed.

In less than an hour, they arrived at the parking area. Caution tape blocked the trailhead and a sign read CLOSED FOR MAINTENANCE. That explained why there were no other cars in the parking lot.

Two officers were holding leashes of what David presumed were cadaver dogs. David had used the same pair last year to find a lost child. A team of officers with jackets emblazoned with the acronym CSI were meeting next to a black SUV.

The Inspector opened the door and helped David out of the back of the car. "We're ready. Lead us to the bodies."

David's heart sank. He used to be a part of this gang, although the people involved in this case were unfamiliar to him. He appreciated that kindness. He plodded towards the empty trail. The Inspector walked beside him in silence.

"We walked in about a quarter of a mile," David said solemnly.

As he hiked, the burden he felt was heavier than the body he had dragged those months ago. He reflected on how his life went so wrong. He'd been a good cop. He'd always been a good cop, until Jack Daniel's came into the picture. The demands of the job drove him to drink. Drinking until he passed out was the only way he could sleep at night. Of course, drinking led to money problems, and money problems led to gambling, and gambling led him to Daniel. He got in over his head, and owed more money than he made in a year. There was no way to dig himself out of the hole he had gotten himself into. That was, until Daniel offered to clean the debt ledger. It wouldn't cost David anything. "Nothing at all," Daniel had assured him.

David only had to look the other way. One hand washed the other. At the time, they both understood David didn't have a choice. Daniel swallowed hard, remembering how screwed up things had been back then. He'd made a deal with the devil. And although he quit drinking, the debt was still there. And the bargain had been sealed with blood.

Inspector Miller broke the silence. "How much farther?"

David looked around, shaken out of his own thoughts. "We're getting close. Then we'll have to veer off the trail to the left for about a third of a mile."

The Inspector nodded. They walked in silence, but the officers trailing them made a lot of noise.

David stopped. He stared at the boulder jutting out of the earth littered with graffiti. "This is it. This is the place where we turned off."

The Inspector signaled to the others that they were leaving the trail. The officers maneuvered over fallen trees and broken branches. Ten minutes later, David announced, "We're getting close."

The Inspector gave the order to release the cadaver dogs. The dogs immediately took off with their noses to the ground. It didn't take long before they pawed at a spot near a pine log.

"This is the place," David said with certainty. The handler gave a command, and the dogs stopped pacing and lay down. "We put this log over the grave to keep the wildlife away."

"Grave?" Inspector Miller asked. "Just one?"

David nodded. "We threw them both in the same grave. What with all the rocks in the soil, it was nearly impossible to dig one grave deep enough. They're down about 6 or 8 feet."

This was the first time he'd been back to the gravesite, and he was amazed at the poor job he and Bobby had done. It didn't take an expert to see the ground around the log had been disturbed. There were bare patches of dirt, as well as disturbed sticks and leaves everywhere.

The CSI team began taping off the area, 20 by 20 feet across. Forensic photographers began taking pictures.

Inspector Miller cautioned the officers, "Before you start digging… we need to collect any evidence we can find off the bodies. Keep that in mind. A fiber, a hair, blood spatter, anything and everything. We already have a suspect in custody--" at which point everyone looked at David. The Inspector continued, "We need the DNA to match, placing him at the scene."

David stood motionless beside the Inspector. He would miss being a cop. Miss being a part of a team. Dammit, why did things have to turn out this way?

He watched as the men in the trench put Vicks VapoRub under their noses. The stench was strong, and others were reminded to do the same. No one offered any to David. The bodies were recovered.

"Jesus," Inspector Miller said, "You just threw them together in one grave."

David said nothing, but his head nodded instinctively. He watched as pictures were taken and evidence was collected. He watched as they placed the bodies carefully into body bags. He watched as 8 men carried the bodies down the trail. David and the Inspector followed solemnly after them.

The men grumbled about the weight, but he could tell they were glad to be away from the gravesite. They were glad to be doing something substantial, not tied to the remote crime scene. David knew the CSI team would be there for a few hours more, maybe even days, before the site was returned to some semblance of normal.

It felt like hours before everything was finished. Before all the evidence from the grave and surrounding area was collected. Before the grave was filled back in. Before it looked serene again.

Inspector Miller and David followed the others out. They sat in the car in the parking lot as the last car drove away.

"What now?" David asked.

"You and I will go to a safe house. The fewer people who know about this part of the plan, the better. If the DNA confirms that Smith is the killer, then we'll see where things go."

"I won't need to stay and testify?"

"I'm not sure. That's for the DA. But maybe not... we've got everything we need to convict him. He's been under surveillance for a while now."

David nodded, and the Inspector continued, "If that's the case, you can do what you want. I suggest you disappear and go wherever you want, just don't stay here or you'll wind up a dead... keep that in mind."

****

The safe house was an off grid, ramshackled cabin in the middle of the woods. It was old, with a couple of cracked windows. The two men went inside. It was dusty and dingy. There wasn't any electricity, but instead an oil burning lantern.

Inspector Miller lit the lantern, and the place looked worse once there was light. An old metal-framed twin bed was pushed up against the wall. It had an old, military-style blanket on top with a flat pillow. There were cobwebs in the corners of the one-room shack. It didn't have a bathroom, but it did have an outhouse.

There was a fireplace in the center of the wall. To the left was an old table that looked like it would fall over at any moment. There wasn't a kitchen or a sink. Instead, there was a plastic bin to hold water.

"You'll have to pump water by hand outside, and there's an old grill outside that you can cook on. You won't be staying long, so I just packed you a few sandwiches in that cooler over there in the corner."

David eyed the cooler. "You wouldn't happen to have a few beers in that cooler, would you?"

The Inspector laughed. "I'm afraid not, but there are a few bottles of water."

David shook his head. "I never saw my life going this way."

The Inspector shrugged. "It's better than the alternative."

"How long will I be here?"

"Just tonight. So, I suggest you ponder where you'll be heading."

David nodded. "What about my wife? She'll be wondering where I am."

Inspector Miller looked out the window for a minute. "I'll tell her the guys on the inside killed you. It's a believable story. The guys on the inside have a severe dislike for cops."

David looked around the small cabin and said, "It's probably better that way. She doesn't need to be involved in the mess I've created. I have about a thousand dollars in cash stashed in my locker at work. I don't suppose you'd be able to get it for me?"

"That won't be a problem. You need anything else?"

"Maybe a pair of clothes. I think it would be obvious that I should be in jail with my Department of Corrections jumpsuit."

"Alright. I'll be back in the morning with some clothes and your cash. You'll be safer traveling by bus. I'll bring you documents for a new identity and drop you off at the bus station in the morning."

****

The next morning, Inspector Miller banged on the door, waking David. "It's time to go. Get up and get ready."

David sat up and rubbed his eyes, trying to erase the horror that had become his life. He looked at the Inspector standing in the doorway.

"What's with the suitcase? Did you get the money?"

"Yes, it's in the suitcase, along with some clothes. You'd look conspicuous if you were traveling without luggage, hence the suitcase. Did you decide where you want to go?"

"I'm going to head out west. Get lost in California. With the millions of people, it shouldn't be hard."

Inspector Miller pulled out some papers and a driver's license. "You are now Jeff Garrow. Here's your license, passport, birth certificate. Everything you need to start over. Are you ready?"

David nodded.

The two men walked out of the cabin and climbed into the car. David didn't look back. He'd never look back. The nightmare for him was finally over. No more Daniel. No more Bobby. A clean slate. He wouldn't screw this up.

Chapter 24

Victoria and Jess arrived at the Macon Bed and Breakfast. As they checked in, Victoria spotted a wine cooler behind the check in counter. "Is the wine for sale? she asked.

"Yes, it is," the clerk responded.

"Can I have a bottle of red?" Victoria asked.

"Certainly."

The clerk reached into the cooler and took out a bottle.

"Can I have a bottle, too?" Jess asked.

The clerk looked back at her. "Red or white?"

"Red, please."

Once the two bottles were purchased and the women were checked in, they made their way to their room. The room was quaint with dark wooden floors and pristine white walls. There were photographs hanging on the walls of the surrounding mountains and farmland. The bed was covered with a red and black plaid blanket. There was a basket of fruit and chocolate sitting on top of the mini fridge.

Victoria plopped on the bed and lay back. Jess looked at her friend. This whole night had been a nightmare, and she just wanted to wake up and start all over again.

Jess popped open her bottle of wine and poured it into two glasses that were located on top of the dresser. She walked over and gave a glass to Victoria, who sat up and took a sip.

"I needed this," Victoria sighed.

Jess agreed. "That was crazy. I can't believe we're still alive," she said, sitting on a small couch and tucking her feet up under her. "And David? Did you know he was in on this?"

Victoria looked sad. "Not really. I suspected, but I learned early on it was better not to know what Daniel was up to. As long as he left my business alone, I was happy." She kicked off her shoes and took another sip. "I don't want to think about David or Daniel for a long, long time," she said sleepily. "Say, what about Peter?"

Jess groaned. "What about him?"

"He's in the hospital, and you didn't go. Are you planning on going to talk to him?"

Jess refilled her glass and took another sip. The wine was finally beginning to relax her. "When I do, it's to tell him I want a divorce. He treated me like I was crazy, and when Bobby had us all cornered, Peter was only looking out for himself. Now that I think of it, most everything he did was for himself. He's a liar. He may not have abused me physically--"

"Like Daniel," Victoria interrupted.

Jess was quiet for a minute, remembering the night when she had stormed into Victoria's house when Victoria was screaming, and Daniel was abusing her.

"I'm getting a divorce," Jess said soberly. Her eyes filled with tears. "I'm getting a divorce. I never thought I'd be saying that. What am I supposed to do now?"

Victoria laughed. "Live. Be free. Be happy."

Jess wiped at her tears. "How do I do that?"

Victoria shrugged. "What would your dream life look like?"

"My dream life?"

"Yes, if you could change your life, what would you do?"

Jess blew out a deep breath. She was quiet and gazed into her glass of wine like she was looking into a crystal ball. "I want to get as far away from here as I can."

"Where would you go?"

"Anywhere that has a beach."

Victoria exclaimed, "Yes! Let's go to Hawaii. It has the best beaches. Have you ever been?"

Jess laughed. "No, I've never been. Peter wasn't one for traveling."

"Let's go," Victoria exclaimed excitedly.

Jess looked at her friend and said sarcastically, "Oh yeah, let's run to Hawaii,"

"We'll put it on the bucket list," Victoria said pragmatically.

Jess stared at her. "Yes, let's!" She burst out laughing again.

****

"Jess, wake up!" Victoria was shaking her, trying to rouse her out of her sleep.

"What?" Jess opened her eyes wildly. "What's wrong?" she said, sitting straight up.

"The money," Victoria said. "We've got to get the money."

Jess shifted her legs over the bed and looked up at Victoria. "What are you talking about? What money?"

"The money in the safe at the store. We've got to get to it before the police do. They're going to come for me. It's only a matter of time. We've got to get the money out."

Jess was wide awake now. "The money from the store? Isn't that yours?"

Victoria shook her head and paced around the room. She started sifting through her clothes, frantically looking for something to wear. "Daniel would launder his drug money through my store. That's what Bobby was after. Now that he's been arrested, he'll lead the cops to me. I've got to get the money out before that happens. You've got to help me."

Jess knew she was in over her head. It made sense that Victoria would be considered an accomplice to Daniel's dealings, but if she helped Victoria, then she'd be an accomplice, too.

"I can't," said Jess. "I can't help you. I'm sorry."

Victoria looked at Jess incredulously. "You're kidding, right? It's because of you all of this happened in the first place. It's because of you that my husband is dead, and my house has become a crime scene. I've been beaten, bloodied, and attacked. My whole life was The Blooming Boutique, and now I'm about to lose that. The only thing I have left is the money. Once this is over, that's my new start, *our* new start. We can go to Hawaii like we talked about. We can get the hell out of here and never come back.

Jess stood up and looked out the window, pondering what Victoria had said. *Could she just leave and never come back. Start over? It was tempting but...* She turned back to Victoria. "I'd be an accomplice too. I would be giving in to Daniel's money, to what he did. I can't do that.

Victoria shook her head. "Fine, stay up on your high horse. See where that gets you."

Both women jumped when there was a knock on the door. It was 3 a.m. There was only one person it could be.

"Police, open up!"

Victoria looked pleadingly at Jess. "Please, please help me. There's an envelope in my purse addressed to you. Read it and it'll explain everything."

Victoria opened the door and let the officers in.

"Victoria Easton, we have a warrant to bring you in for questioning."

Victoria looked at Jess one last time. Her eyes pleading for her help. Then, she turned back toward the officers. "I'm ready," she said.

Jess sat in the empty room, not knowing what to do next.

"Damn it," she muttered. "How did this happen?"

It was a redundant question, she knew. She scanned the small room. How did she go from having a home, a marriage, a life, to having nothing at all? This felt like Daniel's revenge from beyond the grave. She was left with nothing, just like he was. Just like Victoria.

Jess reached for Victoria's purse and found the envelope. She held it in her hand for a long time, debating whether she wanted to open Pandora's box. She lifted the flap and pulled out the paper.

Jess,

Thank you for helping me. This money is our new start.
The combination to the store is 15, 31, 62.
The safe is located
in the back of the store in my office. If you open the closet

you will see the safe. The combination is 21, 16, 32. Once you open it, you can store the money in bags that are on the shelf above the safe.

Once you have the money, call this number 435-6778 and ask for Vinny. He can be trusted and didn't work for Daniel. He's my ex and he's always been there when I needed him. He's got a plane and will fly you anywhere you want to go.

Keep in touch through Vinny and I'll catch up to you as soon as I can.

I trust you. I need you to trust me.

Jess groaned. *Victoria never gives up* she thought, shaking her head. Jess thought about Peter and filing for divorce. What did she really have left? Nothing. Against her better judgment, she started getting dressed. Digging through Victoria's purse, she found her keys. She walked outside, and instinctively looked around, making sure no one was watching her. Jess nervously started the car and drove to The Blooming Boutique.

Once she was parked out front, she turned off the car. Sitting there in silence, she wondered if she was doing the right thing. Opening the door, she stepped out of the car.

Her hands were shaking as she punched in the combination for the door. Once she had entered the store, she turned on the flashlight on her phone to make her way to the back of the store. She didn't want to draw any attention to herself and having the lights on in the store at 3:30 in the morning would have looked suspicious. Once she reached the office, she shut the door and turned on the light.

Jess sat down in the chair at Victoria's desk. She hadn't broken the law yet and could still walk away if she wanted to. The black steel safe was behind the closet door. Could she do it? She looked down at the combination and shook her head, knowing she had lost her mind. Jess stood up and walked over to the safe.

Sure enough, the same duffel bags she had seen being traded at Daniel's were sitting on the shelf above the safe. She took one down and placed it on the floor. She held the lock in her hand and glanced at the paper. In the back of her mind, she could hear herself say "walk away", and that's what she was doing. Walking away from what she had gone through with Daniel and with Peter. Helping Victoria walk away from her past mistakes. They both deserved a new beginning, and that's what they were getting.

Jess's hands were no longer shaking when she entered the first number of the combination. She was sure of what she was doing. She entered the second number. After the last number, she heard the click of the lock, and opened the safe. Never in her life had she seen so many piles of banded one-hundred-dollar bills, along with twenties, tens, and ones. She also found papers listing offshore accounts. She shoved the papers and money into two bags and zipped them up. She carried the bags out of the shop two at a time. Again, she scanned her surroundings, looking for anything out of place.

Once the bags were loaded in the car, she leaned back and breathed a sigh of relief. She had done it. She had gotten the money.

****

It was 7 a.m. when Jess pulled up to Kelly's Kitchen in Lake George. She had just ordered breakfast and taken a sip of her coffee when she saw George walk in. He sat down across from her and smiled.

"You're a sight for sore eyes," he said. "How are you?"

Jess smiled back at him. "I'm good. Better than good, actually."

George studied her. "If you're better than good, then what's this all about?"

Jess leaned across the table at him and whispered, "It's about a ton of money sitting in the back of my car."

George leaned back and sighed. "I've got a pretty good idea where you got it from, but I've gotta ask, did you steal it?"

Jess was shocked. "What? No, I didn't steal it," she hissed.

She opened her mouth to tell George about the money, but he interrupted her. "Don't tell me another word. That's all I need to know."

The waitress came over and delivered Jess's food and refilled her coffee. The waitress looked at George. "The usual?" she asked.

"Yes, ma'am," he said, smiling.

After she left, Jess said, "I don't know what to do next, George. I'm scared."

George smiled at her and replied, "Go live your life, Jess."

"I don't know how. It's always been Peter and me, and then Victoria needed help, and now--"

"Victoria will be back," George said knowingly.

"How do you know?"

"I'm good at what I do, remember? Plus, Wyatt may have had the feeling that you'd come see me and wanted you to know that he's working on a deal."

George took a bite of toast, then a sip of his coffee. "So, where are you going?"

"I don't know. I don't want to stay here. I want to be somewhere far away from all the madness."

"I know just the place," George replied.

Jess took another sip of her coffee, waiting for him to continue.

"Hawaii," he said simply.

Jess burst out laughing. "First Victoria says this, and now you. I'll just fly off to Hawaii. Sure, George, I'll just fly off to Hawaii."

George reached across the table and took her hand. "I'm not kidding, Jess. I have a small bungalow in Hawaii, right on the beach. You can hear the waves at night as you drift off to sleep. It's quiet and a bit remote. You won't have to worry about the neighbors," he said jokingly. "It's the perfect place for you to figure out what you want to do with your life."

A weight felt like it had just been lifted off Jess's shoulders. Hawaii. Why not?

Chapter 25

Jess sat on the beach watching Sampson and Victoria romping in the water. It was a perfect day, but every day that she'd been in Hawaii had been a perfect day. The sunshine was perfect, the bungalow on the beach was perfect, the temperature was perfect, she had no regrets.

She closed her eyes and sank back into her beach chair, her face towards the sun. She listened to the water lapping at the white sand. The seagulls called to one another, diving into the water in search of food. Victoria squealed, and Jess opened her eyes to see Sampson shaking his tail, splashing her.

Off to her right, a little boy was running, holding onto a kite string. The kite swooped back and forth with the current of the wind. A small girl squealed with laughter, running alongside her brother.

She looked to the left and noticed a tall, muscular man walking her way. The bright shorts quickly gave away that he was a tourist. She laughed to herself. Nine months ago, she was the tourist. Now this was home, and she wouldn't trade it for anything.

As the man got closer, he looked vaguely familiar. That was ridiculous. The only person she knew was Keanu, who was the bartender at the local pub she and Victoria frequented. Once she looked into those green eyes, she knew at once who it was. Wyatt.

She stood up and walked towards him. "Wyatt! What are you doing here? How did you find us? I can't believe you're here." She immediately hugged him, and then thought better of it and awkwardly let him go.

He grinned as he looked down at her. "Hi, Jess. You look good. Hawaii agrees with you."

"Thanks. What are you doing here?"

He motioned towards Victoria. "I thought I'd check in on the two of you. Make sure you ladies stayed out of trouble."

Victoria walked out of the water and hugged Wyatt. "Wyatt, what are you doing here?"

He smiled. "Just making sure you're staying out of trouble."

She beamed at him. "Thank you again for all the strings you pulled. I don't know how I managed to get lucky enough to just get probation."

Wyatt shrugged. "You made it easy with good behavior. I'm glad it all worked out, and now you're free to come and go as you please. Just try to stay on the right side of the law from here on out."

Victoria hugged him again. "I will. I swear."

He turned towards Jess. "I have something for you."

"For me?" Jess raised her eyebrow in surprise.

He beamed. "I think you'll like it. Unfortunately, it's back at the hotel. Maybe we can meet up for dinner?"

"I'm intrigued," Jess replied. "I have a better idea. Why don't you come over to our place for dinner?"

He nodded as he bent over to pet Sampson. "I'd like that."

"Great, why don't you come by around seven?"

"Sure, thanks."

"How did you know where to find us?"

Wyatt laughed. "George. He sends his love, by the way."

"Of course, George. I should have known."

"He was the one who suggested I come and see you."

"Really? He didn't mention it when I spoke to him last."

Wyatt shook his head. "That doesn't surprise me. I'll see you at seven."

****

Wyatt rapped on the door at seven o'clock. There was no answer. He walked around the wooden bungalow to the back. In the backyard, the two women were sitting on bamboo chairs, sipping glasses of wine. His gaze went back to Jess. She was beautiful. The orange, floral halter dress she was wearing showed off her tan and my god those bare shoulders. He shook his head. *Where did that come from?* He shifted his head and spotted a fire blazing in the fire pit, and tiki torches around the outside perimeter of the yard. The sound of jazz was playing softly in the background.

He cleared his throat and said, "I knocked, but there was no answer." He stood awkwardly, holding a bouquet of flowers.

Jess smiled and walked over to him. She took the flowers from him.

"Would you like a glass of wine? Or if you'd rather, we also have beer."

"A beer would be great, thanks."

Jess disappeared into the small bungalow and came out with a bottle of beer and a plate of steaks. She handed him the bottle, and then ambled towards the grill. She opened the top and placed the meat on the grates.

Wyatt sauntered over to her. "Would you like some help?"

She laughed and said, "I'm more than capable of grilling us up some steaks. Victoria and I are self-sufficient businesswomen."

"Really?" Wyatt said in surprise. "What business is that?

Victoria strode over and said, "I'm opening up a flower shop on the edge of town."

Wyatt raised his beer. "Congratulations."

He looked back at Jess. "And you? What are you doing?"

Jess laughed. "I'm working for Victoria until I figure out what I want to do. We also have a shack on the beach where I sell leis and hibiscus flowers to tourists."

She adjusted the flame on the grill and led Wyatt to a seat beside the fire.

He was just about to sit down, then changed his mind. He looked back at Jess. "Just a minute, I forgot your surprise." He walked outside to his car and reached into the glove box.

He came back carrying a manila envelope with her name on the front.

"This is for you," he said, handing it to her.

She looked puzzled as she took the envelope from him.

She lifted the flap and pulled out a stack of papers: a divorce decree. She gave an excited yelp.

"What is it?" Victoria asked.

"The divorce is final." She looked up at Wyatt, smiling. "It's over. It's finally over."

She hugged him. "Let's celebrate."

Victoria switched the music to reggae and turned it up. Wyatt took Jess's hand and twirled her around while Victoria turned over the meat on the grill.

Jess danced over to the table and refilled both her and Victoria's wine glasses.

"Dinner's ready," Victoria announced.

Wyatt followed Jess into the bungalow to help her with the plates and silverware. He looked around the place. The walls were wooden, and the floor was a light gray tile. The kitchen was simple, with a few light-colored cabinets and a small stove. She opened one of the doors and pointed to the plates, then she opened a drawer and started taking out silverware.

Once they were all seated at the table, Wyatt held up a glass. "I propose a toast. To freedom."

"To freedom," the women said in unison.

****

After dinner and another bottle of wine, the trio cleaned up the table and settled around the fire. Sampson lay on the ground beside Jess's feet. She gazed at the stars, marveling at how different her life was now. Within a year, she had gone from being married to what she thought was the love of her life to being divorced. She had a dog and a best friend. The bungalow was located at the edge of the beach so she could listen to the waves every night. She couldn't be happier or more content.

Wyatt leaned over towards Jess. "Can we go for a walk?"

She shrugged. "Sure." She smiled at Victoria.

"Go," said Victoria. "I'm going back in the house. It was nice seeing you again, Wyatt."

Wyatt reached out a hand to Jess and pulled her up. She looked down at Sampson.

"Come on, Sampson."

Sampson circled Wyatt and Jess as they made their way to the beach. The full moon made the night feel magical.

"This place is amazing, Jess."

"Yes, it is. Wyatt?"

"Yes?"

"Why are you really here?" Jess asked.

"I told you, I wanted to check on you both and make sure everything is alright. Plus, I'm on vacation," Wyatt replied.

Jess shook her head. "I don't believe you. You would have called first. Tell me why you're really here."

He looked serious. "You never gave me your number."

She giggled and playfully pushed his shoulder.

He stopped walking and looked at her. "Jess, are you happy?"

"Sure, I'm happy. How can I not be? Have you looked at this place?"

He shook his head. "No, I mean just being here selling flowers on the beach. Is that what you want to do?"

She shrugged and started walking again. "No, not long term, but it's good for now. I just got divorced. I survived Daniel's craziness. I need time to decide what I want to do next. Working at the flower shack is what I need right now. What is this all about?"

He chuckled and they stopped walking. He held up his hands in surrender. "You've got me. I'm here for a reason."

She eyed him suspiciously. "What's the reason?"

"I need your help."

"You need help with everything that happened with Daniel? Is the trial not going well?"

"No, no, nothing like that. Actually, I'd like to offer you a job."

"A job?"

The tide was starting to come in, and the waves were beginning to push over the top of their feet, as they resumed walking in the sand.

"Jess, you have a great sense of intuition. You're smart. You know when something's not right. You proved that with Daniel. I'd like you to work with me on a case. It would be undercover, and you'd be working directly for George and me. You wouldn't be working for the FBI."

She eyed him skeptically. "What kind of case?"

"A missing child. A little girl. Her name is Callie."

"What would I have to do?"

"Just be yourself. Meet the family, meet the townsfolk, get the lay of the land. Let me know what you find out. There are certain circumstances where a woman can fit in better than a man. We need you, Jess."

"Can I think about it?"

"Of course, but I want to make something very clear. I don't want you being a hero or putting yourself in danger. You're not a PI, you're just someone who looks trustworthy and friendly and can help us with our investigation. No one can know you are working with us. Not the family or the police. We have some suspicions, but I won't share them with you unless it's pertinent to you or Callie's safety."

"How long has she been missing?"

"Three years. We have a lead in the case. Will you think about it?"

"Yes."

"Yes, you'll think about it?"

"No. Yes, I'll help you."

Wyatt took hand and led her down the beach. She looked up at the sky marveling at how far she'd come. She didn't know what life had in store for her but whatever it was, she was ready.

About the Author

Connie Spanhake lives in upstate New York with her family and her dog. She loves to travel and meet new people.

Other Books by Connie Spanhake

Dark Secrets
Finding Me

Made in the USA
Middletown, DE
13 March 2024